ALSO BY SIMON RICH

Ant Farm

Free-Range Chickens

ELLIOT ALLAGASH

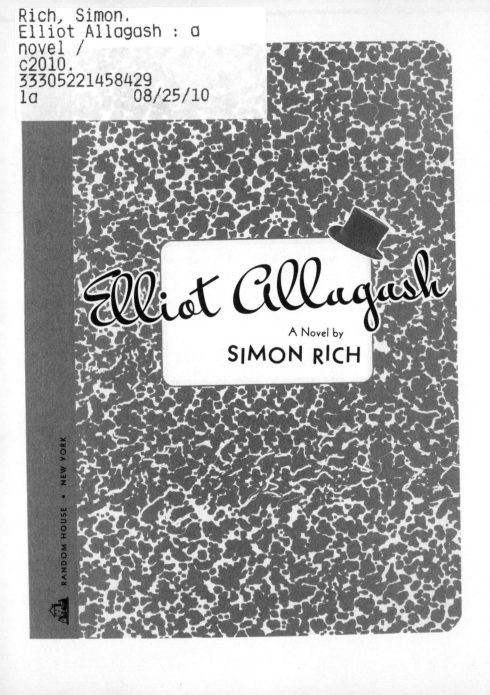

Elliot Allagash

A Novel by
SIMON RICH

RANDOM HOUSE • NEW YORK

Published in the United States by Random House, an imprint of The Random House Publishing Group, a division of Random House, Inc., New York.

RANDOM HOUSE and colophon are registered trademarks of Random House, Inc.

LIBRARY OF CONGRESS CATALOGING-IN-PUBLICATION DATA
Rich, Simon.
Elliot Allagash : a novel / Simon Rich.
p. cm.
ISBN 978-1-4000-6835-7
eBook ISBN 978-0-679-60377-1
1. Preparatory school students—Fiction.   2. Preparatory schools—Fiction.
3. Children of the rich—Fiction. 4. Money—Fiction.   5. Male
friendship—Fiction.   I. Title.
PS3618.I33353E66 2010
813'.6—dc22   2009043885

Printed in the United States of America on acid-free paper

www.atrandom.com

9 8 7 6 5 4 3 2 1

FIRST EDITION

Book design by Simon M. Sullivan

For Jake

CONTENTS

PART ONE

Free Parking

MY PARENTS ALWAYS TOOK my side when I was a kid, no matter how much I screwed up. When I smashed my brand-new Sega Genesis during a temper tantrum, they blamed the game "Sonic the Hedgehog" for getting me riled up. When I lost my passport at the airport, they blamed themselves for entrusting it to me. So when I told them what Elliot had done to me, I was pretty surprised by their reaction.

"Maybe it was an accident," my father said. "Accidents happen all the time."

"I don't think it was an accident," I said.

"Are you sure you didn't imagine it?" my mother asked. "You have such an amazing imagination."

I struggled to resist the compliment.

"No," I said. "It wasn't my imagination. This thing definitely happened."

It was Monopoly night and even though my father had rolled a seven, he hadn't yet moved his wheelbarrow. It just sat there, on the wrong square, abandoned. Eventually, both of my parents got up and went into the kitchen.

"Mom? Dad?"

They didn't respond but I could hear them murmuring to each other on the other side of the door.

"He pushed me down the stairs," I said, for what seemed like the hundredth time of the night. "He pushed me, on purpose, in front of a lot of people. It was really crazy."

Eventually, my parents returned to the table. I noticed that my father was holding a beer. I had only ever seen him drink at weddings and funerals and I was mildly shocked. They both hesitated for a moment, hoping the other one would do the talking.

"The thing about Elliot," my mother said finally, "is that he's different from most boys."

I felt a sudden stab of guilt.

"Oh geez," I said. "Is he retarded?"

"No," my father said. "Not exactly."

"What is it then?" I asked. "What's different about him?"

My mother cleared her throat.

"He's rich," she said.

My father nodded.

"He's *very* rich."

• • •

When I look back on the past five years of my life, which have been dominated by Elliot Allagash in almost every way, I can't help but think about how strange it is we met in the first place. By the time he showed up at my school, in a white vest and boat shoes, Elliot had lived in seven cities, including London, Brussels, and Zurich. Elliot's father, Terry, liked to switch homes regularly, based on his whims. The only reason he had moved the family to New York, according to Elliot, was that his favorite glovemaker had opened up a store on Madison Avenue. The choice of Glendale Academy was far less arbitrary: It was the only private school on the East Coast that would consider taking Elliot as a student. While living in those seven cities, he had gotten himself expelled from more than a dozen top-tier schools. Only Glendale, with its dilapidated gym and dated chemistry charts, was financially desperate enough to overlook his record. By the time I met Elliot, his offenses included vandalism, truancy, unprovoked violence, drunkenness, hiring an imposter to take a standardized test, and blackmail. He was thirteen years old.

It's strange we crossed paths. But it's even stranger that we became best friends.

• • •

Glendale was a small school and it was getting smaller every year. The three long tables in the cafeteria could accommodate about sixty students, but there were only forty-one in my eighth-grade class. When we ate lunch, the twenty most popular kids sat at the back table and the next twenty squeezed into the middle table. I sat at the third table.

Now I'm sure that if I wanted to I could have wedged myself into the middle table—I'd done it once by turning my tray sideways. But the truth is I *liked* the third table. It was spacious, quiet, and, as far as I was concerned, perfectly located. Most students treated lunchtime as a social activity. But I preferred to think of lunchtime as a kind of contest, the goal of which was to drink as many chocolate milks as possible. I didn't consider lunchtime a success unless I had consumed at least five cartons. At any other seat in the cafeteria, this would have been an impossible dream. But by positioning myself within ten feet of the lunch lady, and working closely with her, I could accomplish this feat almost every day.

I was working on carton number three one afternoon when I noticed that Elliot was sitting right beside me. He had no food in front of him, just a large black notebook.

I hadn't seen Elliot since he had inexplicably pushed me down the stairs four days ago, on his very first morning at Glendale. I assumed he had sat down next to me in order to apologize. But by the time I went up for my fifth chocolate milk, it was clear he had no intention of doing so. He never once looked in my direction during the meal. Instead, he just stared at his notebook, noisily scratching the pages with a razor-sharp fountain pen. He sat next to me at lunch the following day, and the day after that, and both times it was exactly the same. He never spoke to me or even looked at me. He just sat there, writing. Sometimes he ripped a piece of paper out of his notebook, crumpled it up, and tossed it onto the floor. And once in a while he snapped his fingers before jotting something down with a flourish. I thought about asking him what he was working on, but it seemed important and I didn't want to interrupt. It didn't occur to me until years later that he might not have been working on anything. All that scribbling

and crumpling and snapping—that was Elliot's way of saying
hello.

• • •

Whenever there was a physical altercation between two students,
both of them got detentions, regardless of who started it. The policy seemed unfair to me, but I didn't see any point in arguing with
teachers. And besides, I didn't really mind detention. It was only
an hour long and Ms. Pearl, the elderly librarian who supervised
it, let us each take two pieces of Laffy Taffy from her bowl at the
start of every session. School felt crowded and claustrophobic, but
detention was usually empty, except for me, Ms. Pearl, and which-
ever boys had attacked me over the course of the week. It was a
peaceful environment and sometimes, during stressful weeks, I actually looked forward to it.

Occasionally, Ms. Pearl made us fill out detention forms, but I
knew from experience that nobody actually read them, so I never
spent much time on them.

Name: *Seymour*
Grade: *8th*
Offense: *Fighting*
Describe what happened: *I was standing by my locker,
humming a song from the radio, when Lance came over and
started fighting me.*
What have you learned from this experience?
*Apparently humming is one of the things that sets Lance off
and makes him want to fight you.*

What could you have done differently?
Nothing.
How do you plan to modify your behavior?
I will try not to hum around Lance.

There was a lot to like about detention: the quiet, the candy. But the best part was that Jessica was there. During the school week, I only caught glimpses of her. She was always surrounded by a buffer of boys who followed her from class to class and blocked her from view. But during detention, that buffer dissolved, and I got a chance to observe her up close.

Jessica earned her detentions by flagrantly violating the dress code, over and over again, in a variety of shocking ways. Her outfits were so obviously inappropriate for school that teachers routinely forced her to change into gym clothes in the lobby before classes even began. If she claimed not to have any gym clothes with her, the teachers would sprint to the Lost and Found and drape her with whatever garments they could find there. They moved with the urgency of firemen struggling to extinguish a five-alarm blaze.

It was astonishing to me how much someone's life could change in just a couple of months. In seventh grade, Jessica had been shy and mousy, a nervous girl whom teachers were constantly reminding to "speak up." But over the summer, everything about her had gotten much louder. Somehow, she had experienced all of the positive effects of puberty and none of the negative ones. Her face had grown angular without succumbing to acne. She'd sprouted several inches, but her teeth had remained perfectly straight. And while certain parts of her body had swelled enormously, she had retained her size-zero frame. Her body had become so obscenely proportioned that even teachers had a difficult time interacting with her. They stuttered or tripped over their words, and occasionally she would have to ask *them* to "speak up."

Jessica never wore a backpack or carried around any objects that would suggest she was a student at our school. At the beginning of every class, a few boys would dash over to her table and lend her the supplies she needed to get through the next forty-five minutes. I sometimes overheard girls call her stuck-up, but they just didn't know her as well as I did. Jessica was just a person, like everybody else. Sure, she sometimes screwed up and wore tube tops or face glitter. But who couldn't relate to wearing the wrong clothes? I knew I could. On two separate occasions, I'd accidentally shown up to school still wearing my pajama bottoms. Was there any difference?

And besides, even if she *was* breaking the rules on purpose, who could blame her? I had never encountered a human like Jessica before, but I had read plenty of X-Men comics and I thought they provided me with a pretty solid frame of reference. In my mind, Jessica was like a brand-new superhero who had only recently discovered her mutant powers. She had to get a crazy costume. It's the first thing you did when you became a superhero.

Even though many months had passed, I still remembered our first conversation. We were sitting in detention at the beginning of the school year when she suddenly swiveled toward me and smiled.

"I'll trade you my Laffy Taffys for a pencil," she said.

"Yes," I said.

It was the longest conversation we had ever had, and I often replayed it in my head.

Ever since that day, I made sure to bring extra pencils to detention in case she needed one. On the face of it, our relationship was pretty superficial: I gave her one pencil each week in exchange for two Laffy Taffys. But there was more going on than a simple economic transaction. I would have given Jessica pencils for free, even if there weren't any Laffy Taffys involved. And I liked to think that she would still have given me her Laffy Taffys, even if I had no pencils to offer her.

We didn't know each other very well, but she always made sure to thank me by name.

"Thanks, Seymour!" she'd say. Or, "Thanks a bunch, Seymour!"

And I'd say: "Of course, anytime!"

It was one of the highlights of my week, right up there with eating the Laffy Taffys themselves.

I was displaying an assortment of pencils on my desk for Jessica to choose from when Elliot showed up to serve his time for pushing me down the stairs. Even though we'd sat together every day at lunch that week, we still hadn't spoken. He was fifteen minutes late to detention, but he moved incredibly slowly.

"Looks like someone needs a watch!" Ms. Pearl said.

Elliot did not respond. I noticed that he was wearing a very large and elaborate watch.

"Well, you still get candy," she said, offering him the basket.

Elliot ignored her and took a seat in the back.

"No candy?" Ms. Pearl exclaimed. "Come on, all boys like candy!"

Elliot looked down at the detention form lying on his desk. After a long sigh, he picked it up and held it out at arm's length, pinching it between his thumb and forefinger, like it was a piece of garbage. As soon as Ms. Pearl turned her back, he loosened his grip and let it flutter to the floor. Then he took out his notebook and started writing.

There were four of us that day: me, Jessica, Elliot, and Lance. Lance hadn't attacked any specific person that week, but he had gotten a detention anyway for "general violence." He was doodling a lightning bolt in the margins of his detention form when his pencil tip broke from the force. He held it up to the light and groaned.

I smiled as Lance rifled through his backpack, looking in vain for a sharpener. Sure, he had me beat in a lot of categories. He was stronger, funnier, more popular, less startled by noises, etc. But when it came to effective class preparation, I could teach him a thing or two. There was a reason why Jessica came to *me* each week for pencils. Because when everything was on the line, she knew she could count on me. And not just for pencils; for erasers, Scotch tape, and whatever else she needed.

Jessica scooped a handful of pencils off my desk and hurried across the room.

"Hey, Lance," she whispered. "Need a pencil?"

She fanned them out in front of his face so he could see them all at once. He stared at them for a while, smirking.

"Can I take two?"

Jessica nodded rapidly and Lance plucked out his two favorites. "Thanks, Jess," he said.

She averted her eyes, embarrassed.

"Of course!" she said. "Anytime!"

She plopped the remaining pencils onto my desk, returned to her seat, and watched in rapt silence as Lance finish doodling his lightning bolt.

Some of my pencils rolled onto the floor, and when I stooped to pick them up, I noticed that Elliot was watching me. He kept staring at me for the rest of detention, even as he unscrewed his pen and flipped to a new page of his notebook.

• • •

My parents rarely asked me how school was going. It's not that they weren't interested; the stakes were just too high. Glendale wasn't particularly glitzy by Manhattan standards. It cost significantly less than those top-tier prep schools that lined Central Park and dotted the hills of Riverdale. But it was still an expensive school—the most expensive one my parents could afford. They never mentioned money around me, but our apartment wasn't very large and if I stayed up late, I could hear them talking about their financial struggles through our shared bedroom wall, in the hushed, low tone they reserved for that subject alone. They were paying an incredible percentage of their income to send me to Glendale and I think they were both secretly terrified that their investment was coming to naught.

If my parents had told me my tuition cost a hundred dollars or a million dollars, I probably would have believed them either way.

Money was meaningless to me until it was converted into rock candy. My father had recently begun to give me five bucks a week to teach me the value of a dollar, but the five-dollar bill he handed me each week might as well have been a voucher with the words GOOD FOR ONE MEDIUM BAG OF ROCK CANDY printed on it, because that's the only thing I ever considered buying with it. When I tried to visualize the amount of money I was wasting by going to Glendale, I pictured myself wading through an entire *roomful* of rock candy, like Scrooge McDuck, scooping up the pieces and tossing them over my head. It felt that obscene.

On the rare instances in which my parents asked me about school, I felt tempted to confess everything: How I was the only student in third-year French whom the teacher had to address in English. How someone had sarcastically nominated me for class president at an all-school assembly, and it had prompted laughter so prolonged and intense that the principal actually had to bang some kind of gavel, which I had never seen before, to make it stop. How I had faked my last four fevers just to have an excuse to stay home and take a break from it all. But I didn't want them to think I was ungrateful. And besides, I had a feeling they already knew about all my problems, even though I never talked about them. They never asked me follow-up questions about school. If I told them the swim test had been "normal" with "no weird things," they took me at my word and allowed me to change the subject. And when I said I had a fever, they never consulted a thermometer. They just squeezed my shoulder, carried the television into my room, and told me to feel better.

Their standards for me were almost unbelievably low. They

congratulated me on Cs and hung Bs on the refrigerator. If I managed to get an A on something, they immediately called my grandmother, even if it was late and she was ill.

"No!" she would exclaim. "I can't believe it! I *don't* believe it!"

"It's true!" my mother would say. "Seymour, tell her!"

"It's true," I'd mutter.

And then she would start screaming, *really* screaming, like the time she won the Mediterranean cruise at our annual synagogue raffle. I appreciated the support, but sometimes I wished that the bar was just a little bit higher.

• • •

One week had passed since Elliot pushed me down the stairs and he still hadn't said a single word to me. He continued to sit beside me at lunch, though, scribbling in his notebook and staring creepily at me from time to time.

I was trying my hardest to ignore him. We had a French vocabulary quiz after lunch and I was determined to do well for a change. I was memorizing the French words for animals when I felt a firm tap on my left shoulder. When I looked over, Elliot was facing me. It was the first time we had ever made eye contact and I was struck by how tired he looked. His face was smooth and unblemished, but the bags under his eyes were dark and craterous. He somehow looked both young and old for his age.

"What's wrong with you?" he asked.

It didn't occur to me until he started speaking that I had never actually heard his voice before. It was high-pitched and lilting, but also weirdly phlegmatic. He sounded like an elderly British woman with a lifelong smoking habit.

"What do you mean?" I asked.

"The bell is about to ring," he said. "And yet you've only consumed two chocolate milks. At this rate, you'll never finish the five cartons you find it necessary to go through during each and every lunch period."

I forced a laugh.

"I don't always drink that many."

"Yes, you do," he said, flipping idly through the pages of his notebook. "In fact, you often drink as many as six."

His eyes widened suddenly.

"On one occasion . . . you drank *seven*."

I looked down at my lap.

"I didn't think anybody saw that."

"So?" he said. "What's the problem? Are you ill?"

"No—just nervous, I guess. You know, because of that French quiz."

He grabbed the textbook from my hands.

"Why are you looking at the animals page? The quiz is on job names."

"When did he say that?"

"He didn't," he said. "But it's obvious."

"What do you mean?"

He curled his fingers and leisurely examined his cuticles.

"Mr. Hendricks never writes his own quizzes. He's too naïve. He always just photocopies them straight out of the book."

"So?"

"So, there are only nine vocabulary quizzes in this chapter. And we've done the other eight in class. There's only one left."

He flipped my book open to the "Occupations" page and handed it back to me. I couldn't believe it. There were five minutes left in lunch and I had neglected the only page that mattered.

"How did you figure all that out?" I asked.

"Basic reasoning."

I started to study the page, but at this point, I was more interested in Elliot's strange book.

"What are you working on?" I asked.

"It's none of your business," he said.

"Oh. Sorry."

I quickly returned to my book. *The farmer, the businessman, the cook—*

"It's research," Elliot said. "I'm doing research."

"Oh, really? On what?"

"I'm afraid I can't tell you that."

He stared at me in silence for a while, until it was clear that I wasn't going to press him for additional information. Then he started talking again.

"My father donated a sizable amount of money to this horrible place and it seems that I'll be forced to stay here for a longish period of time. I'm studying the school to make my time here as painless as possible."

He flipped through his notebook and showed me some of the diagrams he had made. One charted the frequency and duration of fire drills. Another ranked the teachers by seniority. There were detailed maps of the school, including the boiler room and maintenance tunnels, and a few random codes which looked like locker combinations.

"What's this one?" I asked, pointing to a list of students' names.

"It's a status index," he said. "I've been trying to chart everyone's position. See? That's you, at the bottom."

"That's *way* off," I said.

"You think you should be higher?"

"No . . . that part's right. But the rest of it needs some work. Like, Lance should be much higher. You didn't even put him in the top five."

Elliot nodded slowly.

"What else?" he asked.

I scanned through Elliot's list. I noticed that he hadn't put himself anywhere on it.

"Well, you should probably put Jessica higher," I said. "And the bottom's wrong too. Some of these people have lots of friends."

He handed me his fountain pen.

"Fix it," he demanded.

I awkwardly took the pen.

"Okay . . . but, Elliot? Can I ask you something?"

"What?"

"Why did you push me down the stairs?"

Elliot shrugged.

"Amusement," he said. "And research purposes. I wanted to test the extent to which they'd discipline me."

"But why'd you decide to push *me*?"

"In order to standardize the experiment, I needed to commit a generic crime. Abusing you seems to be a pretty common offense around here."

"I guess that makes sense."

"Let me ask *you* a question," Elliot said. "Why are you so unpopular at this school?"

I could tell by his tone that he didn't mean any malice by the comment. He was just genuinely curious.

"You have about as much money as the other children. You're overweight, but not drastically. I mean, some of your classmates are actually obese."

He pointed them out.

"So," he said. "What is it?"

I thought about my unpopularity more or less constantly, but I had never actually had a conversation with anybody about it.

"A lot of reasons," I said.

"For instance."

"Well, for instance . . . I'm not so great at sports. Especially basketball."

Elliot's eyes widened.

"Status is determined by *athleticism* here?"

I nodded.

"That's a big part of it."

"So that black child who's always jumping up and down to touch the tops of things—"

"Chris."

"Whatever. That boy is considered powerful? Even though he's obviously on scholarship?"

"People don't really care about stuff like money at Glendale," I explained. "It's more about how cool you are and how good you are at sports and whether or not people think you're stuck-up. Stuff like that."

"Is that what you really think?"

Elliot closed his eyes and massaged his temples, like talking to me had exhausted him. His limp blond hair, so fair it was nearly white, fell over his hands. He smoothed it back, opened his eyes and pointed at me.

"Has anybody ever told you that money trumps everything? That nothing else in this world matters?"

I shook my head stupidly.

"I could buy you all the popularity in this school," he said. "With a little research and some well-placed investments, I could make you a *king*. Admired by girls, respected by boys, feared by all."

I laughed nervously.

"What would I have to do?"

Elliot grinned.

"Everything I say."

• • •

When I tell people stories about Elliot, they always ask me the same question: Why did he devote so much time and effort to improving your life if he barely knew you and the two of you had just met? It's a good question. And the only way I can even begin to answer it is by talking about video games.

Before I met Elliot, I played *a lot* of video games every day after school. And even though I wasn't crazy about playing basketball in real life, I was thrilled when my parents gave me NBA Slam '97. The game was unique at the time because it allowed you to become the "coach" of a team. You could make trades, sub in players, and play an entire season against the other teams, all of which were controlled by the computer. I set the game to "easy" because it was my first time playing. And I chose the Sacramento Kings, because I liked their uniforms—purple and black with a slash of silver.

The computer suggested a starting lineup based on who the five best players were in real life. But I decided to use my coach status to mix things up. Mitch Richmond, a six-time all-star, was slated to start at guard. But that was what everyone was expecting! I decided to take him out of the lineup and replace him with Derrick Phelps, a random benchwarmer who had only played in three official games during his entire professional career. As soon as I entered the change, a line of red text appeared on the screen:

Are you sure you want to substitute DERRICK PHELPS for MITCH RICHMOND?

I hesitated for a moment, aware that I had made an unorthodox coaching decision. But then I got angry. Who was the computer to tell me who I could and couldn't put into my starting lineup? I was coach of the Sacramento Kings! I spitefully hit the start button, and within seconds, Derrick Phelps was making his way onto the court. I won the tip-off, passed him the ball, and immediately made him fire up a three. It was a horrible shot, barely grazing the rim, and the other team easily got the rebound. Had I made a mistake? I decided to call a time-out and take a closer look at Derrick's stats from the previous season:

Games Played: 3
Total Minutes: 5
Points per Game: 0.0

They weren't very encouraging, especially when compared to Mitch Richmond's numbers for the same year:

Games Played: 82
Total Minutes: 3172
Points per Game: 22.8

I switched Mitch Richmond back in for a couple of plays. He immediately got a steal and threw a no-look alley-oop pass to my center. The crowd went wild, but their cheers left me cold. It was too easy to dominate the game as Mitch Richmond. Sure, I could play by the book and let him carry my team to a championship. Or I could turn the basketball world upside down and create a new legend from scratch. A legend named Derrick Phelps. I called another time-out and put him back in the game.

By the end of the third quarter, Phelps had taken nearly seventy three-pointers. He was programmed to miss the majority of his shots. But he had still managed to rack up sixty-six points, and with the game on "easy" mode, it was all we needed for a victory.

Within three weeks of steady after-school playing I had led my Sacramento Kings to a world championship. By that time, Derrick Phelps had broken every important record in the history of the NBA. He finished the season averaging eighty points a game. And he never missed a single minute of action, no matter how obviously fatigued his body became.

Every night while lying in bed, I imagined myself inside the game, holding a press conference as coach of my electronic Sacramento Kings.

"Where'd you discover this Derrick kid? He's the next Michael Jordan!"

"He's *better* than Jordan," I'd say. "He's doing things in this league that have never been done before. Things that have never been dreamed about."

"Do you have any problems with his shot selection? Last night he attempted thirty-seven three-pointers, including nine from behind the half-court line. Isn't that the mark of a selfish player?"

"You listen to me," I'd say, pointing angrily at the imaginary reporter. "Phelps has brought more fans to this league than any player in its history. If he wants to shoot sixty-footers, well, I think he's *earned* it."

When I found Derrick Phelps, he was an inexperienced player with no respect in the league, and within one season, I'd transformed him into the most dominant superstar the sport had ever known. He was my greatest achievement.

I never told Elliot about any of this, but I think he would have understood. Of course, Elliot never played any video games himself. He didn't have to.

• • •

I knew Elliot's proposal was insane. Popularity wasn't something that could be bought, like a pair of sneakers. It took *years* to acquire, or if you were Jessica, one physically intense summer. It was fun to imagine being popular: sitting wherever I wanted at lunch, playing two-player video games, humming without fear of violence. But those were just fantasies and my time at Glendale had taught me not to dwell on them.

Besides, my situation wasn't nearly as dire as Elliot had suggested. Sure I wasn't popular in the traditional sense, but people still respected me. In fact, I had just been invited to the most important social event of the year: Lance's birthday party. The invitation had come a few days late and I had spent a whole weekend in panic mode, convinced I was one of the few people he'd left out. But eventually my mother had presented me with the glossy red card, signed by Lance himself. How bad could things be? I had been "cordially invited" to "Lance Cooper's Slammin' Swim Party." As an afterthought, maybe. But who cared? Lance *wanted* me there. And that was honestly enough for me.

I dreaded the event itself, of course. I hadn't appeared in front of my classmates in a bathing suit since the seventh-grade swim test. And the memory of that event was so terrifying it literally caused my face to sweat. On the morning of the party, I would almost definitely feign illness to avoid having to go. But that was beside the point. Lying awake in bed, with Lance Cooper's invitation propped against my windowsill, I felt a contentment I hadn't known in months. It was the first party I'd been invited to since enrolling at Glendale. And who knew? Maybe my life was starting to turn around.

I was about to fall asleep when an unmistakable odor drifted into my bedroom. My mother was baking something—something delicious. I instinctively hopped out of bed and groped my way down the darkened hall. It wasn't until I saw the kitchen clock that I realized something was amiss. My mother *never* baked this late at night.

The kitchen was completely dark except for the faint, yellow glow of the oven light. I looked around for my mother, but she had gone into her bedroom to wait out the baking process. I peered into the oven incredulously. It didn't make any sense: My mother was making cookies—an entire batch of peanut butter cookies—and I hadn't been informed. I was about to knock on her door and confront her when I caught sight of a tin box on the counter. My mother had lined it with wax paper and attached a thank-you card to the lid. It was addressed to Mrs. Cooper.

Lance's mom.

I flipped open the card.

Thank you so much for agreeing to include Seymour, he couldn't be more excited! As per our discussion, I will make sure Seymour is aware of proper pool hygiene and that there won't be a repeat of the swim test "incident."

I slunk back to my room, queasy with shame. My father had seemed so thrilled when I told him about Lance's party at dinner. I wondered if he knew about my mother's pathetic intervention—and the preconditions she had agreed to. I could picture Lance arguing with his mom for three long days before reluctantly signing my invitation. I could picture him eating the cookies with his friends, explaining their sad origin.

It was eleven at night, way past any reasonable kid's bedtime, but somehow I knew that Elliot would be up. I locked my door for the first time I could remember and quietly looked up his number in the directory.

"Okay," I said. "When can we start?"

Elliot laughed.

"Immediately."

• • •

"So, Vlad, you never played in the National Basketball Association?"

"Well . . . no. Not officially. But I practiced with the Pacers one summer, and I played with NBA players in the CBA."

Elliot rolled his eyes.

"You'll have to do," he said.

The basketball player stared down at Elliot with huge, unblinking eyes. Vlad was probably the tallest person I had ever met and his limbs were frighteningly muscular. But he spoke with the quiet nervousness of a boy introducing himself on his first day of school. He dribbled his ball against the hard wood and the echo reverberated all around us. Elliot had rented out an entire YMCA and it was completely empty except for me, Elliot, and Vlad.

Elliot hadn't told me where we were going after school; he'd just pushed me into the back of his limo. I asked him a few questions on the ride over, but he had been too absorbed in phone calls to respond. When we got to the Y, he tossed me a bag of gym clothes—but otherwise he ignored me.

He was wearing a double-breasted gray suit with a blue hand-kerchief poking neatly out of one of the pockets.

"When does the coach select his roster?" he asked.

I shrugged.

He took out his cell phone and pressed a single button.

"Find out the exact date of Glendale's eighth-grade basketball tryouts," he told somebody. He closed the phone and put it back in his pocket.

"Well?" he said. "What are we waiting for?"

For the next hour or so, Vlad subjected me to a variety of bas-ketball drills to assess my "skill level." The first time I dribbled the ball—hurling it against the floor with two shaky hands—he gasped. He tried his best to remain professional, offering me po-lite encouragement after every botched layup, but I could sense the horror on his face. I'd later find out that Elliot was paying Vlad based entirely on my performance. If I failed to make the eighth-grade basketball team, he would forfeit a staggering amount of money.

After my second coughing fit, Vlad cut the drills short and walked me over to the bleachers. Elliot was engrossed in some kind of military history book—naval, from the looks of it—and it took us a few tries to get his attention.

"Well, how is he?" Elliot asked.

"He's not bad," Vlad said, forcing a smile. "He's got heart."

Elliot snapped his book shut and pointed his tiny index finger at Vlad's face.

"Don't bullshit me!" he shouted.

He waited a few moments for the echo to subside. Then he continued in quiet, measured tones.

"This isn't about 'feelings,' Vlad. This isn't about 'self-esteem.' This is about victory. I'm *paying* you for victory. Now give it to me straight: Can you train him to make the team? Or will I have to find somebody who can?"

Vlad sat down on the bleachers.

"Okay," he said. "To be honest? It's not going to be easy. This kid looks like he's never played the game before, or even *seen* it played. And it's not just his skill level. He's a total mess, physically. For a fourteen-year-old, his lung capacity is *really* poor. And his gait . . . the way he runs . . . it's crazy. When he first ran onto the court, I thought he was making some kind of joke. But he wasn't. That's actually how he runs."

Elliot nodded.

"Okay," he said. "So what's it going to take?"

Vlad looked up at the rafters and let loose a long sigh.

"I'd say a *minimum* of two hours a day. Plus strength and conditioning. But that would just be for fundamentals. Without other players to scrimmage with, he's not going to have a real sense of how the game is played."

"Fine, we'll get some other players."

"How are you going to do *that*? I mean, you can't just get an entire squad of—"

Elliot's eyes narrowed.

"Here's a thought," he said. "*You* stop telling *me* what I can and cannot do. Did someone tell you about my situation? Who I am, how I operate, that sort of thing?"

Vlad nodded.

"Okay," Elliot said. "Okay."

He closed his eyes and massaged his temples.

"I'm sorry for yelling before," he said. "I'm in a foul, black mood."

He patted Vlad on his giant shoulder.

"Good work today."

He flicked open his cell phone and whispered something into the receiver. A few seconds later, the gym doors opened and some frustrated middle-aged regulars filed onto the court.

"The court is now open to the public," Elliot announced, wearily buttoning his long, black overcoat.

One of them started to ask him who he was and how he had managed to book their usual time slot, but his friends quieted him down. They sensed, somehow, what a mistake it would be to question Elliot.

• • •

"Tell them that you've been practicing," Elliot said. "Tell them you've been working hard all summer and you want to join in their game."

It was a Friday afternoon and Lance had organized his usual three-on-three game in John Jay Park. Most of the boys were clustering by the court in the hope that they'd get picked this week.

The girls were sitting on the bleachers eating French fries and pretending not to watch.

"What are you waiting for?" Elliot demanded. "Do as I say!"

I explained how hard it was to get one of the six slots, how even the best athletes in the eighth grade had to kiss up to Lance all week to be considered. There's no way they'd select me, I told him, and even if they did, the game would be an embarrassment. I'd definitely made progress in my first five weeks of training: I finally understood what a double dribble was, and, judging from how much dessert my mother was offering me each night, I had lost a considerable amount of weight. But I still wasn't anywhere close to being at their level.

"They won't let me play," I said. "You don't know how it works."

Elliot took two quick steps away from me and then sharply spun around.

"Okay," he said. "For starters: Don't you ever tell me that I don't know how a thing *works.*"

He paused for a moment, to let that sink in.

"You're going to have to trust me," he said. "My plan is too elaborate and ingenious for you to comprehend right now, but it is vital that you follow every step anyway. Now go over there and say, as loudly as you can, that you've been practicing basketball over the summer and that you wish to be selected."

Elliot seemed adamant. I took a long swig of Pepsi to buy myself some time to think. As a rule, I tried to limit my contact with Lance. He had recently started to call me "Chunk-Style," and I was terrified that if he uttered that nickname a few more times it would enter common usage. Then again, Elliot had done so much for me in the past few weeks—I didn't want him to think I was ungrateful. I put down my soda and started to walk toward the court.

"Wait!" Elliot whispered. "Who's that alpha girl holding court on the bleachers? The smiley one with the stupid, *stupid* curls?"

"Oh, that's Jessica," I told him. "She's the one I told you to rank higher on your list. She's probably the most popular girl in the whole grade."

"That's right," Elliot said. "They all look the same to me."

He pointed at me.

"Make sure she hears."

When I came back thirty seconds later, my cheeks were flushed and my eyeballs burned with tears.

"How did it go?" Elliot asked.

"He called me Chunk-Style and everybody heard. I can't believe it . . . people are going to start calling me Chunk-Style. I'm Chunk-Style now. This is now my life."

I looked across the playground. Someone passed Lance the ball and he immediately made a three-pointer. Elliot grinned and returned to his book.

"Why are you smiling?" I said. "He said *no*. It didn't work."

"Are you kidding?" he said. "It worked perfectly."

• • •

Vlad handed me a basketball and manipulated my arms and legs until they were in the proper shooting position.

"Follow through this time," he said. "And don't forget about the backspin."

I checked my grip, bent my knees, and let loose from the foul line. The ball slid off my fingertips, arced through the air, and whooshed through the middle of the net. I swiveled around to catch Elliot's reaction, but he was too engrossed in his book to notice.

"Hey, Elliot!" I called out. "I made a foul shot!"

Vlad laid his giant palm on my shoulder.

"It's way too early to celebrate, kid," he said. "We still got loads more work to do."

Vlad blew his whistle and a tall man in mesh shorts and a baseball cap walked through the doors of the gymnasium. He looked familiar, but I couldn't immediately place him.

"I've brought the children you requested," he announced in a deep, monotone voice. "If you need any more, just let me know."

"Oh my God," I said. *James?*

It was Elliot's limo driver, the guy who drove us to the gym each day. I had never seen him without his black suit and cap.

James snapped his fingers and a group of boys ran into the gym, wearing matching T-shirts. There were exactly nine of them, I noticed, just enough for a full-court scrimmage. Vlad stared at James for a moment, shocked that he had abducted so many children so effortlessly. Then he cleared his throat, blew his whistle, and went back to work.

• • •

"How did you get those kids to come?" I asked on the limo ride back to my apartment.

"I had James create a basketball league," Elliot told me. "There are more than one hundred players."

"Jesus," I whispered. "Isn't that a lot to ask of your driver?"

"James is more than a driver," Elliot said.

"Okay," I said. "But . . . still . . . isn't it a little crazy to start a whole league, just for me?"

"You needed scrimmage partners. And this was the only way to get parents to send in their children. Any other method would have made them suspicious."

"So . . . are there, like, games and stuff? Even when I'm not there?"

"It's a standard league," he said. "There are tournaments, coaches, a newsletter. The team you scrimmaged with today believed they were here for a regular practice. They're called the Timberwolves."

We drove for a while in silence.

"Hey Elliot," I said. "Did you see the fourth quarter?"

"No," he said. "I was reading."

"Oh. Well, it was pretty cool. I stole the ball a couple of times and I made a bunch of layups. I wasn't the best one out there, but I was definitely better than average. I don't want to get my hopes up . . . but I'm actually starting to feel okay about tryouts."

Elliot nodded.

"Don't get too complacent," he said. "The Timberwolves are the worst team in the league."

• • •

Over the next few weeks, my speed increased, my shot improved and my confidence soared. Every week, I played against increasingly better teams in Elliot's league, and by the week of tryouts, I was regularly leading the ragtag Timberwolves to victory.

My mother, terrified by my recent weight loss, had two different doctors test me for parasites. When I tried to explain that I had been playing basketball after school, with Elliot, it only confused her more.

"Didn't he push you down the stairs?" she asked.

"That was just an experiment," I said.

We left it at that.

I wanted to play in the park to see how I stacked up against my classmates, but Elliot ordered me not to.

"Lance might notice your improvement," he said. "And it's imperative that we catch him off guard."

He shook his head suddenly in disgust.

"The fact that someone of Lance's class has *influence* at this school is a perfect testament to its baseness."

"What do you mean?" I said. "Isn't Lance . . . you know . . ."

"Isn't Lance *what?*"

"Well, you know . . . isn't he rich?"

"Of course not," he said. "His father owns some warehouses in Queens. That doesn't exactly constitute an empire."

"But he's got the new Penny Hardaways," I said.

"Exactly! The most ostentatious shoes on the market. He *has* to wear them, to prove that his family can finally afford them! He's like a caveman with a piece of ivory through his nose. Sure, Lance is proud of those shoes. But when his children see photographs, they'll be embarrassed that their father had to *try* so hard. And his grandchildren—they'll be downright mortified."

I looked down at Elliot's shoes. They were hand-stitched loafers made out of what appeared to be alligator skin. They had silver tips and golden buckles and their soles were the color of blood.

"What about *those*?" I asked.

Elliot shrugged.

"The Allagashes have come full circle."

...

Lance may have been the first boy in class to wear Penny Hardaway sneakers, but by the day of tryouts, so many boys had started copying him that he felt the need to upgrade. He was wearing the new Air Jordans—an obscenely priced shoe with gold-plated laces and some kind of removable sleeve. No one noticed them until study hall, when he cocked back his chair and propped both feet up on his desk.

It was a pretty disruptive gesture, but Mr. Hendricks kept his mouth shut. Hendricks was a nervous man, a frail French teacher whose hands shook comically when he yelled. He wore tweed jackets and dark-framed glasses but he couldn't hide the fact that he was the youngest teacher at our school. It was clear from the neatness of his exams, the care he put into his recycling murals, and the way he winced when students complained about the homework. Elliot mocked him incessantly—particularly for the low quality of his tweeds—but he was easily my favorite teacher. He was the only one I could relate to.

Jessica and Lance started whispering and Mr. Hendricks took out a book, pretending he didn't notice. When their voices grew too loud to ignore, he went to the bathroom so he wouldn't have to yell at them.

"You should check out tryouts," Lance told Jessica.

"I've got cheerleading."

I was sitting right behind them; I noticed that at some point Jessica had propped her feet up next to his.

"You guys could get a head start on the season," Lance said. "Cheer me on today."

She inched her feet closer to his, until they were practically touching.

"I'll be there."

My stomach tightened. I was already nervous enough without the threat of female witnesses. If Jessica went, all the girls would. I'd been training for months—what if it all ended in disaster? The only thing that calmed me was the sight of Elliot. He was gazing out the window, arms folded, a serene smile on his face. As hard as it was to imagine myself succeeding, it was even harder to imagine that Elliot could fail.

• • •

A few hours before tryouts, Mr. Hendricks took us over to the playground for recess. I was running through some yoga stretches Vlad had taught me when I heard a commotion by the water fountain. A tall man wearing a giant foam Butterfinger costume was handing out Nestlé product samples. I instinctively began to run toward him when I felt Elliot's hand clamp down on my shoulder.

"It's for them," he said. "Not you."

I looked across the playground. Mr. Hendricks was urging the students to "just take one!" but it was too late. Lance had already organized some kind of eating contest, and the other boys were cheering him on, loudly chanting his name. The man in the foam costume emptied the rest of his sample crate onto the ground and the larger boys began to wrestle over them. Then he nodded once at Elliot and was gone.

"Oh my God," I said. "Was that *James*?"

Elliot leaned against the jungle gym and stared at the crowd.

"Look at the animals," he said. "Eating their sugar."

He looked at his watch.

"Sometimes it's almost too easy."

• • •

Mr. Hendricks usually had to turn off the lights to get us to pay attention to Final Announcements. But an intense sugar crash had settled over the classroom. Most of the class was slumped over in their seats, breathing slowly and heavily, with their eyes half-closed. A few were actually asleep.

"I know everyone is excited for basketball and cheerleading try-outs," Mr. Hendricks said. "But before dismissal, we have a quick student announcement. Elliot?"

Elliot walked over to the blackboard and pressed his hands together, as if in prayer.

"Every year," he said. "Three dozen inner-city youths fall victim to asbestos poisoning. I have decided to start an after-school program devoted to fighting this terrible epidemic. I will serve as president, but I will need a secretary to help me with administrative duties on Tuesdays, Thursdays, and Fridays. Obviously, anyone elected to this position would have to forego any basketball or cheerleading commitments. But I'm sure we can all agree that such a sacrifice is a small price to pay to help remove asbestos from our inner-city schools. I'm asking you, my fellow Glendale Lions, to select the student you deem most worthy of this position."

Few people looked up as he walked around the classroom, placing ballots on everyone's desks. I'd spent enough time with Elliot to grow habituated to his oddness. I was used to his knobby fingers, scratchy voice, and chilling stares. But my classmates treated him like a ghost, ignoring him whenever possible

"I didn't know you were starting a club," I whispered when he sat back down next to me.

"I'm not," he said.

I had more questions to ask him, obviously, about James and the candy, but I decided to leave the matter alone. There was something else I wanted to say to him, something I'd been meaning to say for months.

"Hey, Elliot. Listen . . . even if I don't make the team, I just want to say, like, thank you for—"

He cut me off.

"Don't thank me," he said. "Remember, I'm not doing this out of *kindness* or *generosity*. I'm doing this purely for sport. It's an intellectual exercise—a way to occupy my days during this hellish period of my life."

"Okay," I said. "But still . . . I just wanted to say thanks. It really means a lot to me."

Elliot hesitated and fiddled with his cuff link. It was the first time, I realized, that I had ever seen him look uncomfortable.

"You're welcome," he muttered finally.

The bell rang and we filed in to the gym.

• • •

The tryouts seemed to move in slow motion, like something out of a dream. I had improved so much so rapidly that it felt as if everyone else had gotten worse. I stole the ball from Lance at the first possible opportunity and bulleted across the court for an easy layup. Lance, a little bit shocked, did his best to score on me during the very next play. But I anticipated his crossover move, stole the ball again, and broke free for another layup. I shot this one left-handed, for variety's sake. Meanwhile, Elliot's sugar blitz was having the desired effect. The other boys were so sluggish on the court that the coach actually stopped practice during a sprinting drill to give a speech about "desire." One of the larger boys, who had been eating samples pretty steadily since recess, took this opportunity to run into the bathroom and vomit.

In the beginning of the tryout, when I first started dominating, Lance responded with laughter. But his amusement quickly gave way to frustration—and then fear. During the final seconds of the scrimmage, he and another boy double-teamed me at the half-court line in a desperate attempt to stop me. I got past Lance with a spin move, threw the other defender with a pump fake, and knocked down a three-pointer at the buzzer. The gym fell into a reverential silence. The only sound I could hear was a thin, high-pitched giggle coming from the bleachers. I assumed it was one of the girls—they were assembled in the front row—but it was Elliot. He was sitting alone in the very last row, drinking what appeared to be some kind of martini. He grinned at the stunned cheerleaders, nodded at me once, and then was gone.

• • •

I wasn't aggressive enough to fight my way through the crowd, but I didn't have to see the list to know I'd made the team. A few boys who I barely knew patted me on the shoulder and even Lance mumbled his congratulations. I was about to head home when Elliot stopped me. I threw out my arms to hug him—but he held up his palms in protest.

"We're not done yet," he said.

"What do you mean?"

"The goal wasn't to get you onto some pitiful athletics team," he said. "That was only a stepping stone. We're not after acceptance; we're after dominance."

He leaned in close and continued in a whisper. His breath was foul, like the formaldehyde we used in frog dissections.

"Trust me," he said. "This is only the beginning."

He stood up on a chair and addressed the mass of students huddled around the list. The results for secretary were in, he said, and by a large majority, the class had selected me. My new teammates stared up at him in shock.

"He can't do it," one of them said. "He made the basketball team."

"I know the sport of basketball is very important," Elliot said. "But this is a chance to help underprivileged children. Maybe we should let him decide."

The boys scoffed and jeered. But the girls, I noticed, had a different reaction. Some of them were rolling their eyes at the boys. And some of them were smiling at me with a far-off look in their eyes.

"What are you going to do?" Jessica asked me, laying her hand on my forearm. *"Which one are you going to choose?"*

There was a popular series of books that year called Magic Eye. Each book contained a bunch of computer-generated images. The pictures were meaningless, but if you stared at them long and hard enough, you started to see three-dimensional shapes. A horse, a crown, a sword. This was that moment, when the blurriness finally cohered into a shape and I started to get the picture.

I waited until all eyes were on me. Then I cleared my throat, paused for effect and announced my decision.

"I've decided to join Elliot's club," I said. "The basketball team might be more fun, but I'd rather make a difference in the world."

I could hear the girls talking excitedly as I followed Elliot out into the street. I managed to contain my excitement until the limo doors were closed.

"Did you see when Jessica touched my arm? *Did you see?"*

"I saw."

"Did you see the look on Lance's face?" I said. "When I bailed on the team? Oh my God . . . it's like I'm too awesome to even *play* with that guy! I'm too awesome to even be on his stupid little team!"

"You've got it, Watson."

"I guess there's no asbestos club, huh?"

"Of course not. But we're still going to meet three times a week."

"What for?"

"To plot our next move. We came out sprinting, but we're still nowhere near the finish line."

He opened the sunroof, flooding the car with heat and light. I poked my head out and a rush of wind cascaded over my face. I imagined for a moment that there was no limousine—that it was just *me* on Park Avenue, sprinting uptown at thirty miles an hour. I shouted for Elliot to join me, but he refused. Eventually, after a few blocks, I grabbed his scrawny wrist and yanked him up off his seat. He struggled and cursed for a block or two, like a fish on a hook, but when his head emerged through the sunroof and the warm air hit his face, he looked at me and broke into an involuntary grin.

"Pretend there's no car!" I shouted, pumping my arms in place. "That it's just us running!"

I looked so ridiculous doing it that we both burst into laughter.

Elliot ducked back into the limousine.

"James, pick up the pace!" he said. "Can't you see we've got work to do?"

• • •

If there's one thing I've learned from television, it's that you should never trust a genie. It doesn't matter how you spend your three wishes. The genie will always find some way to screw you. If you wish for a million dollars, it'll come in the form of a life insurance claim after your wife dies in a plane crash. If you wish for fame, a mob of fans will trample you to death.

"I thought you said you wanted money?" the genie will say, a smirk on his smug genie face. "I thought you said you wanted fame?"

"Not like this!" you'll scream. "Not like this!"

And the genie will laugh at you, his muscled, blue arms folded self-righteously at his chest.

When I was ten I saw an episode of *The Twilight Zone* about a shopkeeper who discovered a genie. When he wished for power, he was *immediately* transformed into Hitler. That seemed a little unfair to me, even by genie standards. But, of course, I placed the blame squarely on the shopkeeper. He shouldn't have wished for something so selfish and petty. He should have been content with his humble shopkeeper's existence. He should have remembered all the cautionary tales he had read as a boy about genies and their treachery, and when he spotted that golden lamp and rubbed its smooth, sleek surface, when he smelled that purple smoke and heard that booming voice, he should have just thrown it away.

That was easy for me to say. At the time, I had never met a genie.

• • •

Elliot had a great toy collection. He had an entire shelf of bug fossils. He had an old version of Monopoly from the 1930s, with a circular board and crumbling bills that peaked at "Twenty Dollars." He even had a coin-operated genie—a life-size, turbaned automaton in a glass box, named The Great Shamba. If you slid a nickel into the machine, the genie gyrated for thirty seconds and a card slid out of his mouth like a paper tongue. The cards all said the same thing: IF YOU INSIST.

Elliot's bedroom had a dumbwaiter, which was hooked by a pulley system to a central kitchen. I never once saw the kitchen, but it must have been heavily staffed. They were able to produce any dish he requested, no matter how elaborate. Whenever Elliot wanted anything, he scrawled his order onto a scrap of paper, tossed it into the box, and lowered it using a large circular hand crank that looked like the steering wheel of a ship. A bell would ring several floors below to signal his order's arrival, and within thirty minutes the crank would begin to turn in the opposite direction. The aroma of food would slowly waft up the shaft, growing in intensity until the dish itself materialized. Elliot rarely ate anything besides watercress sandwiches, but he encouraged me to test the kitchen's limits. I tried dozens of strange dishes on Elliot's recommendation: steak tartare, clams Casino, beef Wellington. If I didn't like something, he would scribble down another order, spin the wheel, and try again.

The dumbwaiter was designed for food, but Elliot used it for all sorts of purposes. If he grew bored of his outfit, he would send down for "an array of jackets" and a shipment of freshly wrapped clothes would promptly arrive. He'd try them on in one of his many full-length mirrors, keep the ones he liked and toss the rest back down. Once, when I tried to start a homework assignment during one of his lengthier stories, he ripped the math worksheet out of my hand and tossed it into the dumbwaiter. The answers arrived within minutes, along with a separate document "showing the work."

Sometimes Elliot sent down for objects that he had misplaced around the house, like his fountain pen, phone, or keys. All he had to do was jot down what was missing and turn the magic wheel. The bell would ring, followed by some rustling noises, and before long the misplaced object would reappear in Elliot's hand. When he was especially bored, he hid his keys in a remote location—under a bureau, say, or behind a tapestry—and timed how long it took his staff to locate them.

The Allagashes hadn't been able to find a residential building that was large enough to suit their needs, so they'd moved into a former courthouse that they had purchased from the New York City government. They'd gutted the interior but left the façade intact: columns, flags, and all.

What Elliot referred to as his "bedroom" was actually a cluster of several rooms spread out over two floors. He had an office, a dressing room, some kind of film library which he kept locked, and two walk-in closets. He also had a billiards room, which contained a second, smaller dumbwaiter. That one he used exclusively for drinks.

The most incredible thing in Elliot's house was the gigantic bear that his father had shot and then had mounted inside his library. The bear was at least a foot taller than Vlad and three times as wide. But it wasn't his size that I found shocking; it was his pose. The bears I'd seen in museums looked ferocious, with their forearms outstretched menacingly and their toothy mouths set into permanent growls. But this bear didn't look tough; he looked terrified. His eyes were wide and watery and the prickly hairs on his scalp stood straight up in the air. His paws were raised defensively in front of his face. I imagined Elliot's father following the trail of blood, stalking the wounded bear to the place it had chosen to die. The bear was frozen at that moment, when the hunter had aimed his gun to finish it off with a final, fatal shot.

There was also a stuffed monkey in the front hallway, wearing a tuxedo. Elliot had shot it with his father on his last trip to Africa. It was small, about the size of a human kindergartener.

"Give Jeeves your coat!" Elliot commanded the first time I passed it.

I looked down at the monkey. Its scrawny back was hunched over in a deferential bow and its waxy lips had been bent into a horrible grin. Its right arm was thrust out to receive coats.

"I don't want to," I said.

Elliot laughed.

"Don't be impolite," he said. "Jeeves is waiting."

"I'll just hang it up somewhere else," I tried.

Elliot stopped laughing, and we stood there in silence until I finally agreed to drape my purple windbreaker over the monkey's stiffened arm.

• • •

Elliot chalked the end of his cue, squinted at the table, and effortlessly knocked a ball into the corner pocket. He had brought me to the billiards room to teach me how to play, but in forty-five minutes, I had taken only three shots. Elliot was running the table.

"Tell me more about this Jessica girl," he said. "Does her power stem from money, sex, or both?"

"Jesus," I said. "I don't know. People just kind of like her."

Elliot's eyes narrowed.

"Money, sex, or both?" he repeated.

"I guess . . . sex?"

"Interesting."

I nodded confusedly and changed the subject.

"This pecan pie is great. The guy who makes desserts down there is really awesome."

"It's three guys, actually. They're all pastry chefs, but they have different specialties."

"Wow," I said. "That's amazing."

"You're lucky you can still experience pleasure. I've become accustomed to a level of decadence so extreme that to go without luxury for even a minute fills me with a powerful rage. A rage that you could never understand."

"Oh," I said. "Well . . . just be sure to thank those guys for me, okay?"

Elliot sighed.

"Okay."

He racked the balls and prepared to break again.

"Hey, Elliot?" I asked. "Who's that guy in the painting? Riding the horse?"

"That's Terry," he said. "I suppose you should meet him at some point."

"Who's Terry?"

Elliot hesitated.

"My father."

He smacked the white ball with surprising force and a couple of striped balls skittered into the side pockets.

"Would you like to meet him when he's drunk or sober?" he asked.

"I don't know. What do you think?"

Elliot shrugged.

"It's your call. Terry's more entertaining when he's drunk, but he's also less predictable. More prone to outbursts."

"I think I'd rather meet him sober," I said.

"Then we better hurry," Elliot said. "It's almost four o'clock."

• • •

I followed Elliot down the stairs and into the bright-green library. Terry wore a red monogrammed bathrobe and held an unlit cigar. He was slightly balder and significantly fatter than he appeared in his portrait. He was looking intently at the bear, and it took him a moment to notice our presence. When he finally saw us, he bounded over to shake my hand.

"So, you're Seymour!" he said. "Elliot told me about your basketball prowess. And your *valiant* community service efforts."

I started to stammer something about asbestos, but Terry mercifully cut me off.

"It's a miracle that scheme paid off," he said, chuckling. "So needlessly complicated!"

He turned around and rooted in his desk drawers for a lighter.

"What can I say? *Aux innocents les mains pleines,* right?"

I noticed that Elliot's ordinarily pale face was mottled with a splash of crimson.

"What does that mean?" I whispered.

" 'Beginners' luck,' " he muttered.

Terry started to offer me a drink, but a buzzer sounded before I could respond.

"Excuse me," he said.

He pressed a button on his desk and James's voice sounded over the intercom.

"Hodges is waiting outside," he said. "Should I let him in?"

"Yes!" Terry shouted.

Moments later, a disheveled old man shuffled into the room.

"Should we come back later?" I asked.

"Stick around," Terry whispered. "This won't take long."

He stuck out his hand, and Hodges hobbled across the library as fast as he could to shake it. The old man shook our hands as well and then sat down across from Terry. I followed Elliot over to a leather couch on the far side of the library.

"Are you sure your father doesn't want us to leave?" I whispered.

Elliot rolled his eyes.

"He wants us to watch," he said.

Terry sunk into his chair and clasped his hands behind his head.

"I saw your new paintings at the Guggenheim," he told Hodges. "I liked them."

Hodges laughed nervously.

"Of course, I'm no critic," Terry continued, "just a collector. Still, they weren't bad. Some really pretty colors—especially that squiggly one."

"Those are old paintings," Hodges said, blushing. "They're just putting them up now. I haven't done many new paintings lately. Or, at least, not many that can be exhibited."

"Did you get the last payment?" Terry asked.

"Yes," Hodges said. "I did."

"Good!" Terry said. He poured himself a glass of port and took a large sip. I looked at my watch and noticed that it was exactly four P.M.

"I want you to paint a duck," Terry said.

Hodges nodded wearily and took a notebook out of his pocket.

"Any particular kind of duck?"

Terry scrunched up his eyes and drummed his fingers against his desk.

"A happy duck," he said, finally. "Wearing some kind of hat."

Hodges nodded.

"A duck with a hat," he said.

"I'd also like another one of your ambitious ones. You know . . . *abstract*. Like the fuzzy one of the ocean."

"*Green Waters?*"

"Yes—that's the one! *Green Waters.*"

"That reminds me," Hodges said. "Have you by any chance had time to consider . . . my proposal?"

Terry squinted, genuinely confused. He clearly heard a lot of proposals.

"Remind me?"

"I asked if it would be okay . . . if we exhibited *Green Waters.* You would get all the proceeds, of course, since it's *your* piece. I just . . . I feel very strongly that it's my most successful painting in recent years and . . . I would . . ."

"Oh," Terry chuckled. "*That* proposal."

He poured out another glass of port and handed it to the old painter.

"I'm sorry," he said. "It's just not possible."

"I'd be willing to do any number of complimentary paintings to replace it," Hodges said. "Please, sir."

Terry laughed.

"Did James tell you about my situation? Who I am, how I operate, that sort of thing?"

"Yes, of course."

"Then why are you debating me?"

Terry closed his eyes and massaged his temples.

"You know, it's funny," he said. "If you hadn't told me how *good* that painting was, I might have given it up. It would be in some museum by now—or *willed* to one, at least."

Hodges swallowed.

"Do you really plan on destroying them *all?*"

"Yes," Terry said. "They're my paintings, and I'm the only one who gets to look at them. Upon my death, they will be destroyed by my associate James, along with the rest of my Personal Museum."

" 'Personal Museum'?"

Terry's eyebrows arched with incredulity.

"You didn't think you were my only artist, did you? Give me a break! I've got dozens."

"Did you make the same . . . arrangement . . . with all of them?"

Terry grinned.

"Most had the presence of mind to demand more money," he said. "But yes."

"Why?" Hodges asked. "Why would you do a thing like that?"

Terry leaned forward.

"Do you remember when they found that new Van Gogh twenty years ago, at that yard sale? It was in all of the papers."

Hodges nodded slowly.

"Well, that's what got me thinking," Terry said. "I read that article as a young man and thought, 'My goodness. There is nothing more decadent than *unseen* art.' I mean, just think about it! Any collector can surround himself with pieces that are famous or ancient or good. But who owns pieces that will never be seen by other humans? Probably no one since the pharaohs! Do you know how many historians have begged me for glimpses of my collection? How many scholars have tried to sue me for 'robbing humanity of its treasure'? *That's* power—not your name on some plaque in some museum! My collection isn't simply valuable, you see. It's *priceless*."

He leaned in closer and continued in a whisper.

"And it isn't limited to paintings, Hodges. I own sculptures, prints, photographs, films. I owned a novel once, by a Pulitzer

Prize—winning author. It was profoundly beautiful—one of his best. I made him write it for me in longhand, while under surveillance, to make sure he couldn't save it electronically. It cost me more money than you would ever dream to guess. He knew he was surrendering all of his rights to me, but I think he assumed I was planning to publish it someday, on some kind of personal press. He didn't know I planned on destroying it. When he handed me the manuscript and I told him what I was going to do to it, he wept like a child. He offered to return his fee, plus his meager life savings. It was pitiful. I read his book in a single sitting and then burned it in my fireplace, right over there, behind my bear."

Hodges's face was drained of color.

"My God," he said. "What was it about?"

Terry threw back his head and laughed.

"Wouldn't *you* like to know!"

• • •

Elliot led me back into the billiards room and picked up the game where he had left off. When he was finished beating me, I asked him a question that had been on my mind for some time.

"Elliot? What does your father do?"

Elliot repeated the question to himself, as if trying to make sense of it.

"Oh!" he said, finally. "You mean his *profession*."

He laughed.

"He's never worked a day in his life."

"So what does he do all day?"

"He spends money and drinks."

"Is he . . . a philanthropist?"

Elliot shook his head firmly.

"Absolutely not. My family only gives money to charity when it's absolutely necessary for tax purposes. And even then, we only give to foundations that are trying to cure diseases the Allagashes are genetically predisposed to, like hemophilia and gout. There's the Allagash Prize, I guess, but I wouldn't exactly call that charity."

"What's the Allagash Prize?"

"It's a kind of academic scholarship that Terry set up at his old club at Harvard. Every year, it goes to the senior who received the lowest cumulative grade point average while still managing to graduate. The winner is paid in alcohol."

"Jesus!" I said. "But—if he doesn't have a job—what does he *do* all day?"

Elliot shrugged.

"He likes magic. Sometimes, he'll hire a magician to come over and perform illusions for him. While he's eating lunch . . . or in the bathroom."

"How often does he do that?"

"Often," he said. "He doesn't like to be tricked, though. So usually, at the end of the session, he'll pay the magician however much extra cash is necessary in order to get him to reveal his secrets."

"What *else* does he do?" I asked breathlessly.

"He meets with lawyers. To fend off lawsuits and escape punishment for his crimes."

"What kind of crimes?"

I could tell Elliot was getting annoyed by all my questions, but I couldn't stop myself.

"Conspiracies, mostly."

"What kind of conspiracies?"

Elliot smacked his tiny fist against the billiards table suddenly.

"Look—anybody can do what Terry does! Okay? He has no elegance. It's all just *brute force*! He's never pulled off an artful scheme in his life!"

He sat down next to me and sighed heavily, exhausted by his outburst.

"That reminds me," he said. "I've been meaning to ask you something."

"What?"

"How would you like to be class president?"

I laughed. My life at Glendale had definitely gotten easier in the past few weeks. Since basketball tryouts, Lance had stopped fighting with me, or at least had toned down his attacks. And while the nickname Chunk-Style still elicited laughter, it no longer drew applause. That said, I was in no position to run for public office.

"How would you do *that*?"

"Just answer the question," Elliot said. "Yes or no."

I shrugged.

"Sure," I said. "Why not?"

• • •

I swept my fork across my plate, trawling for any remaining shreds of brisket.

FREE PARKING • 55

"Are you still hungry?" my mom asked. "There's one more slice."

"Oh, no thanks," I said. "I'm full."

"What about you, honey?"

My father waved his arms in the air.

"I'm stuffed, love. Why don't you take it?"

My mother shook her head.

"I'll just wrap it up," she said.

My father and I nodded. All of us wanted the brisket, but this ritual of offering one another the final slice was a very important part of our week. We were all obsessed with brisket and relinquishing the last piece was probably the most loving gesture we could make to one another. There was always a soggy slab Saran-wrapped in our fridge, a testament to our family's powerful bond.

I started to talk about my day, to distract myself from the meat, and before long, I had announced my candidacy for class president.

"I think it's great!" my father said, after a long, shocked silence. "Even if you don't win, it'll be a really fun experience."

My parents continued to praise me for a while, making sure to qualify all their compliments with "even if you don't win."

"I'm pretty sure I'll win," I told them.

"Are there . . . other people running?" my mom asked, gently.

"Yeah," I said. "But Elliot offered to be my campaign manager."

Whenever I mentioned Elliot's name, my parents glanced anxiously at one another. They were thrilled that I had finally found a close friend. But they were also frightened, because that friend was Elliot Allagash.

"Wow!" my mom said. "Between basketball and this, you're really spending a lot of time with Elliot!"

I nodded.

"Is he going to help you make posters?" my father asked.

I tried to picture Elliot squeezing Elmer's glue onto a piece of construction paper.

"I don't think he'll help with posters," I said. "But he's good at . . . planning things."

My father looked at me.

"What kinds of things?"

I shrugged.

"Just . . . things."

My parents shared another look.

"Dad? Where did Elliot's dad get all of his money?"

"From *his* dad."

"But where did *he* get it?"

My father laughed.

"From *his* dad."

"But where does it all come from? Do they own buildings, like Lance's family?"

"Oh, sure," my dad said. "They own entire companies."

"But that's not where the money *comes* from," my mom said.

"Right," my dad said. "Those are just things they bought with it."

My mom shook her head softly.

"It all comes from that patent. Right? Just that one little find."

My father twisted his paper napkin into a coil and nodded.

"Just that one little find."

• • •

Cornelius Allagash was born on the South Street docks in 1775, just minutes after arriving in New York City. His mother was nine and a half months pregnant, according to legend, but the unborn capitalist refused to emerge until he had landed on American soil.

Cornelius's parents were hardworking Dutch cobblers. They failed to make enough money to send their boy to school, but Cornelius was bright. He learned to speak English by attending free sermons in City Hall Park. And after swiping a Bible from a lecturer, he taught himself to read. Before long, he had started a successful bootlegging business, selling his moonshine for two shillings a jar.

By the age of twenty-one, Cornelius had amassed enough shillings to buy himself a horse. But his prospects were limited; his house was only large enough for a single still, and it took him nearly a month to produce each barrel. Desperate to get ahead, Cornelius bought some rudimentary chemistry books and attempted to speed up his brewing process. He experimented with different chemical combinations, testing out batches on his horse. But every single trial ended poorly. One day—Christmas of 1800, according to his autobiography—Cornelius became so dizzy from the fumes that he passed out. As he collapsed, he dropped a wooden bucket into the still, smacked his head against a stone wall, and crumpled onto the basement floor. He was unconscious for a few minutes, and when he came to, he couldn't find his bucket. The vessel had vanished. He was beginning to doubt his sanity when he noticed something strange inside his still. The surface of his whiskey-chemical mixture was coated with a thin layer of brown fiber. He ladled out a scoop and examined it by candlelight; it had the consistency of grain, but the softness of sand. His bucket, it seemed, had been pulverized on contact.

Cornelius didn't know what had happened, exactly, but he knew his latest chemical might have value. Anything that could break down wood so efficiently had to be useful to somebody. The city, after all, was clogged with dilapidated tenements and running out of space all the time. You couldn't destroy them with fire; the entire city could go up in smoke. Maybe this chemical could help clear the brush down by the Bowery. There was so much wood in the city, piled into clapboard houses south of Wall, to say nothing of the sprawling forests north of Fourteenth Street. Something that turned it into something else, even mush, had got to be worth something.

In order to patent the chemical, he had to scientifically classify it. So he hired an alcoholic schoolteacher—one of his best clients—to analyze it, in exchange for a jar of moonshine and one percent of any profits that resulted from the discovery. The schoolteacher asked for two jars of moonshine in lieu of the one percent, but Cornelius wouldn't relent. He didn't have two jars to spare. After a fair amount of arguing, the schoolteacher spent five minutes scrutinizing the substance—it was calcium bisulfite, i.e. $Ca(HSO_3)_2$—and signed his name on the dotted line. Today, his progeny are among the richest people in North America. His great-great-grandson lives on a private island in the South Pacific and is rumored to have a personal brothel with more than seventy full-time employees.

Cornelius Allagash forgot about his little experiment, gave up chemistry, and opened up a tavern in the Bowery. Then, five years later, a hardworking German tinkerer thought to press Cornelius's pulp into sheets and let it dry. He was amazed: The sheets retained the strength of wood, but they were polished and smooth. The wood levels could be adjusted to change the sheets' thickness; dye could be added to change their color. They looked like the linens you found in a rich man's bed or the smooth fabric you found in a minister's Bible. But this material was so cheap to make, you wouldn't even have to go to church to see a Bible anymore. You could make your own.

Cornelius Allagash had invented paper.

From that date forward, every paper manufacturer in the western world had to pay the Allagashes for the privilege of turning wood into pulp. Elliot's family owned a small percentage of every cardboard box in existence. They owned a portion of every envelope, a fraction of every baseball card. They made money when people wrapped gifts and collected every time they used toilet paper. They made money from ticker tape parades, whether they took place in Times Square or Nazi Germany. They made money when Japanese schoolchildren sent paper cranes to flood victims and when lonely people wrote their suicide notes. They made money off of every page of every book ever written—textbooks and comics, pornography and Bibles, fat city phone books and little girls' diaries. The Allagashes made money whenever anybody jotted down notes or signed a bill. They owned wallpaper and Kleenex, magazines and newspapers, cards and checks and stamps.

They even owned money itself.

• • •

Elliot carried around a leather-bound book in his breast pocket. It was small but very thick, and its edges were frayed from use. The cover was solid black, except for a single word that had been stitched onto the center with golden thread: *Enemies*. Elliot rarely laughed, but when he did, it was usually while looking though the pages of this book. Terry had given it to him as a present for his seventh birthday, and he had kept it on his person ever since.

Sometimes, after hearing some news from James on his cell phone, Elliot would take out his book and make a check mark next to one of the names listed inside, using a tiny silver fountain pen he kept specifically for this purpose. He made these check marks slowly and deliberately, as if savoring the gesture. It was a terrifying book and I'll never forget the first time I saw it.

Elliot's first act as my campaign manager was to organize a celebratory lunch.

"Shouldn't we wait until we've won?" I asked.

Elliot ignored me and dragged me outside to his waiting limo. He barked out an address, and James sped us over to a windowless midtown restaurant with giant brass doors. Elliot hopped out and motioned for me to follow.

"What is this place?" I asked.

"It's the Winchester," Elliot said. "The most exclusive restaurant in Manhattan, if not the world."

Elliot had lent me his largest suit for the occasion, and it was so tight, I could only take short, shallow breaths. We had changed beside each other in his private dressing room, and it had been a disturbing experience. I knew Elliot was the skinniest kid in the grade, but I didn't know *how* skinny until I saw him without his shirt on. When he bent over to slip on his socks, I could count all the vertebrae in his spine. And when he reached up to grab his waistcoat, I thought I could see his rib cage pulsing in time with his beating heart.

He checked his cuff links, and mine, and led me into the Winchester's mahogany vestibule.

"We could just go to a regular place," I pleaded.

Elliot flashed me one of his more intense and terrifying stares. I took a deep breath and followed him to a table in the back.

"This is an historic location," Elliot told me. "All of the great New York candidates launched their runs from this room! Boss Tweed, Handsome Jimmy Walker . . ."

He continued to rattle off names until the maître d' approached. He was a grim-looking Frenchman with a carefully groomed moustache.

"I'll have a watercress sandwich," Elliot told him. "Seymour?"

I could feel my armpits prickling with perspiration. How could I order when they hadn't even brought over menus?

"Just order whatever you want," Elliot whispered.

"Anything?"

Elliot nodded casually.

"Okay," I said. "I'll have a cheeseburger with onion rings."

The maître d' laughed.

"We don't serve *cheeseburgers*," he said. "Or onion . . . *rings*."

He pronounced the words like they were bodily secretions.

"Oh," I said. "Sorry."

I could feel the blood rushing to my face. I started to stammer out an order for a watercress sandwich—I knew they had that—but Elliot waved his hand in the air.

"No," he said. "You wanted a cheeseburger."

He turned to the maître d'.

"Are you telling me you won't serve *my* associate the items he requested?"

The maître d' sighed.

"This isn't McDonald's," he said.

Elliot's eyes took on a strange sparkle.

"So you're denying him a cheeseburger?" he asked, his voice spookily soft. "And you're denying him onion rings."

"Jesus," I whispered. "Elliot, it's okay. I'll order something else."

"You will *not*," he shouted.

People at other tables turned to face us; we were the youngest customers in the room, I noticed, by about forty years.

"I'm afraid I'm going to have to ask you to leave," the maître d' said.

"Very well," Elliot said. "We'll leave your establishment. But first, I'll take one of your business cards."

He walked over to the maître d's desk and removed a card from a small silver tray.

"And leave you one of mine," he said.

Elliot didn't hold a position at any of his father's companies, beyond the informal title of "heir." But he had a business card all the same, consisting of his name—*Elliot Allagash*—and nothing else. He took one out of his pocket and laid it faceup on the reservation book. Then he grabbed my elbow and yanked me out into the street, into the back of his waiting limo.

"What the hell was that about?" I asked.

But Elliot wasn't listening. He was cheerfully copying the maître d's name and number into his little black book.

"Drive," he said.

And the car roared crazily down the avenue.

• • •

Elliot didn't come to school for a while. The teachers told us he was hospitalized with tropical parasites, but I knew where he really was: at home, plotting his revenge on the Winchester. I didn't see or hear from him until two weeks later, when his limousine pulled up to my bus stop after school. The other kids watched silently as James rolled down his tinted window and motioned for me to get inside. Elliot was waiting for me in the backseat. He was wearing a silk bathrobe, and he had an unusually serene expression on his face. I asked him how he was feeling, on the off chance that he was actually sick.

"Go to the Sun," he told James, ignoring my question. "Let's see about that late edition."

James drove to the Sun Building, ran inside, and emerged seconds later with a crisp new copy of the paper. He handed it to Elliot, who plucked out the Food and Dining section and laid it in my lap. It was still warm from the presses.

"Page three," Elliot said.

WINCHESTER FETES NAZI

When Dan Lubecki was released from prison on Wednesday, most New Yorkers shuddered. It's been twenty years since the self-proclaimed "Nazi Crusader" planted a homemade bomb in Temple Ephraim, destroying one of the city's most celebrated houses of worship. But for most New Yorkers, the wounds have not even started to heal.

In a printed statement, the mayor expressed "frustration" at Mr. Lubecki's release and pushed for tougher hate-crime legislation. Congressman Nathan Stein of Brooklyn organized a candlelight vigil to honor the memory of Temple Ephraim and send a message to Mr. Lubecki that he "was not welcome in the great city of New York." But apparently, Mr. Lubecki still has a few friends left in this town.

Last night, patrons of the venerated Winchester restaurant were treated to one of the most tasteless and baffling spectacles in the history of New York City dining. At approximately 7:55, an overweight man in a clip-on tie strolled up to the maître d'. Few people recognized the man as Mr. Lubecki. He has gained a significant amount of weight since his face last graced the tabloids and his trademark "Hitler mustache" has long since been replaced by a full beard. But when the guest proudly announced his name, heads began to turn. Most patrons averted their eyes, bracing themselves for an unpleasant scene.

"I was sure they would throw him out," said one longtime Winchester patron. "The man is a self-described Nazi."

But Mr. Lubecki was not denied a table. Instead, the maître d' and his assistant personally escorted him to their legendary "fireside booth," an exclusive slot typically reserved for movie stars or royalty. Over the next two and a half hours, the maître d' personally served the Nazi an elaborate feast, consisting of fourteen courses with wine pairings. At one point, Mr. Lubecki began to smoke a cigar, in clear violation of the restaurant's smoking policy. When guests complained that the pungent cigar was interfering with their dining, the maître d' ignored them and placed a silver ashtray by the Nazi's champagne flute.

At the end of the meal, the chef came out to shake Mr. Lubecki's hand and ask him if there was anything else he could offer him. When Mr. Lubecki requested a cab, the chef phoned for one personally and helped the wobbly Nazi out the door. No bill was ever presented.

The scene was so flabbergasting that at first this reporter assumed she had made some kind of mistake. The Winchester, which did not admit women until 1979 and has still never hired an African American waiter, has always been perceived as a somewhat intolerant institution. But no one has gone so far as to call its management Nazi sympathizers.

A quick interview under the awning of the Winchester confirmed that the man was in fact the same Dan Lubecki who was released from prison on Wednesday. When politely pressed for proof, he happily displayed several forms of identification, including his prison release papers, which he proudly carries in his jacket

pocket. He had been invited to dinner by the maître d'
himself, he said, just hours after vacating his cell.

"That Winchester place isn't bad," he said. "They sure
know how to make a guy feel at home."

When I finally looked up from the paper, Elliot was sipping
champagne from a tall glass.

"Would you like a drink?" he asked.

"No thanks," I said. "I have math homework."

Elliot drained the last of his champagne and immediately re-
filled his glass.

"Did you . . . do this?" I asked, gesturing vaguely at the newspaper.

Elliot closed his eyes and held the warm newspaper to his face,
like it was a beloved puppy or kitten.

"Elliot, it really wasn't that big a deal! I mean, you didn't have
to—"

He raised his index finger to silence me.

"Elliot?" I asked. "How did you do this?"

He pressed a button and the sunroof retracted, enveloping us
in warm light.

"Have you ever heard of Alston Bertels?" he asked.

"No, who's he?"

Elliot sighed.

"I'll take it from the top," he said. "No interruptions."

• • •

I had never heard of Alston Bertels, but apparently most New Yorkers had. He was the reigning food critic for *The New York Times* and had been for more than thirty years. In eight hundred words Bertels could transform an obscure noodle house with empty tables and faded menus into the most coveted reservation in the city, with celebrity clients and lines around the block. And he routinely closed down restaurants with a single, cutting review. He always ate under an assumed name, to avoid preferential treatment. And in recent years he had begun to wear a disguise, just in case a clever maître d' kept his photograph on hand.

On Tuesday, three days after Elliot's expulsion from the Winchester, he had James call the restaurant. Speaking in a whisper, James told the maître d' that he was an intern at *The New York Times* and that Alston Bertels would be coming to the Winchester in the near future. He had reviewed it favorably thirty years ago, James told the spellbound maître d', and he wanted to see if its quality had remained consistent. In exchange for a complimentary meal, James said, he would tell the maître d' which assumed name Bertels planned to use and the disguise he planned to wear. The maître d' promptly agreed to the proposal.

"He's coming on the twenty-second," James whispered. "He'll be wearing a full beard. And he'll make the reservation under the name Dan Lubecki."

The maître d' hesitated.

"Like . . . the Nazi? Who's getting out of prison?"

"Yes," James said. "Alston has an unusual sense of humor."

The maître d' asked James to repeat the information to make

sure he had heard it all correctly. Then he asked him for his name so he could arrange his complimentary meal.

"I can't tell you that," James said. "If anyone finds out I leaked this, I'll get fired."

"Well, I'll need to put *something* in the reservations book."

"I understand," James said, reading the final line of Elliot's script. "Just call me 'Hal Sagal.' "

• • •

"Hal Sagal? Who's that?"

Elliot wrote it down on a cocktail napkin, with large spaces between the letters. It took me a while, but eventually I was able to rearrange them.

"Oh," I said. *"Allagash!"*

"I know, I know," he said. "Anagrams are trite. But you want to know something? *You have to know your audience.* I swear to God—anything more subtle would have been lost on him."

• • •

James, posing as a disgruntled Winchester waiter, called every gossip columnist in town. He told them that his bosses were Nazis, and that they had invited Dan Lubecki to spend his first night of freedom in twenty years at their restaurant. Most of the columnists were unable to get reservations in time to witness the event, but a few of the more prominent ones were able to finagle tables. After the columnists had been contacted, the only person left to call was Lubecki himself. The Nazi was skeptical at first, but by speaking in an Alsatian accent and quoting Hitler several times,

James was able to convince Lubecki that he *was* in fact the maître d' of the Winchester and he *did* in fact want him as his guest. Unsurprisingly, Lubecki had no other social plans for the evening and happily agreed to attend.

James called the Winchester once more time, using a British accent this time, to make a reservation on behalf of a "Mr. Lubecki." The maître d' did his best to act natural, but his excitement was obvious. He sounded, James reported, like a first-time gambler calling a large bet with aces in his hand.

• • •

"We'll hit the *Daily News* next," Elliot said, "then the *Observer,* the *Post,* and the *Times.*"

We made the rounds in silence. I was too shocked too speak, and Elliot was too exhausted from his efforts. Every few minutes, James stopped the car, fetched a tabloid, and laid it on top of the stack that was rapidly accumulating in the backseat. But Elliot didn't bother to read them. He only moved once on the ride home: to take out his black book and silver pen and make a little check mark with his tiny, pale hand.

• • •

As far as I knew, the ninth-grade class president didn't have any official duties beyond posing for a picture in the yearbook. But it was a prestigious position, something colleges "looked at," and several weeks at the end of eighth grade were devoted to campaigning.

For the past three years, class president had been a two-person race between Lance and a girl named Ashley. It was usually pretty lopsided. Ashley always won the support of the math club, and one year she had convinced the foreign-exchange student to campaign for her, but everyone else tended to pull for Lance.

"Tell me more about your opponents," Elliot demanded. "Who are their enemies? What are their weaknesses?"

I glanced across the cafeteria. Lance was leaning back in his chair, but he still towered over all the other boys at his table. He'd recently begun to gel up the front of his hair. It resembled a shark's fin and made him look even taller than he was already. He was shouting out catchphrases from a movie he had seen recently and everyone around him was laughing hysterically.

"Well, Lance is pretty funny," I said. "And he's also really cool."

I looked at Ashley. She was at the edge of the second table eating apple slices and studying for a French vocabulary test with color-coded flash cards. Whenever somebody made a joke, she looked up from her flash cards, and her halting, nervous laugh invariably silenced the table. People rarely made fun of Ashley, but they tried their best to ignore her. Whenever she said anything, her hands started shaking and her eyes grew wide with panic. It was stressful just to watch.

She wore her auburn hair in a single braid that was so painfully taut it resembled a length of rope. Lance occasionally yanked on it, causing her eyes to well up with tears. It was a doubly cruel gesture, since it also landed her in detention for "being involved in an altercation." I always felt terrible when Ashley shuffled into Ms. Pearl's classroom, her eyes downcast to avoid Lance's smirk. My detentions never bothered me. Even if I wasn't responsible for any of my fights, I was sure I had done *something* over the course of the week to merit punishment. Ashley was completely innocent, though, and her sentence was an outrage. I never told her I felt this way, but once I gave her half a Laffy Taffy, and I think she grasped the import of the gesture.

"Ashley's not so popular," I said. "But she's probably the smartest girl in the grade. I thought she had a chance last year, because Lance didn't put up any posters or write a speech. But then at the last minute Lance promised a new scoreboard, with a Glendale lion on it, and everyone voted for him. He never got us one, but it was still an awesome idea. West Side Prep has one with a tiger on it and they're always bragging about it at games."

Elliot nodded.

"Do either of the candidates have any physical defects?" he asked. "That haven't been publicly exposed?"

"Geez," I said. "I don't know."

"What are their sexual histories? Have either of them been involved in any scandals?"

I shrugged.

"Don't worry," Elliot said. "James will dig up something."

• • •

After school, Elliot led me into a room I had never seen before, on the fourth floor of his house. It was completely empty, except for a single couch. The walls were bare except for a framed note on the wall directly across from the couch:

Dear Mr. Allagash,

*I apologize for my insensitive comments at the Derby. I did
not mean to disparage your horse.*

    Sincerely,
    John D. Rockefeller

"It's one of my family's most treasured possessions," Elliot told
me, with unusual reverence in his voice. "It was mailed to my
grandfather in the twenties."

I walked over to examine the note up close, but I couldn't figure out why it was so valuable. I knew Rockefeller was a famous
billionaire, but how much could his autograph be worth?

Elliot continued, clearly sensing my lack of enthusiasm.

"Do you know how many letters Rockefeller wrote in his lifetime?"

I shrugged.

"A hundred thousand," he said. "At least. But do you know
how many of those were apologies?"

I shrugged again.

"One," Elliot said. "Just one."

He sat down on the couch and stared at the letter for a while in
silence.

"Hey, Elliot, do you think we should maybe get started on
posters? Lance already put one up and it's pretty funny. There's a
picture of Austin Powers, but it's Lance's head on the body. He's
saying, 'Oh, behave!' "

Elliot did not respond.

"I've discovered some facts that I think you'll agree are of interest," he said. "Lance has a variety of reading-related learning disabilities. He's barely passing most of his classes. And yet he's managed to maintain an A-plus average in history, his most reading-intensive course. How does one account for the inconsistency?"

"Lance has learning disabilities? How'd you find that out?"

"I had James make me duplicates of everyone's files," he said, gesturing casually at a cardboard box behind the couch. "Students and teachers."

"Oh my God," I said.

"Congratulations on the French quiz, by the way, you scored a 91."

"Really?" I said. "Wow. That's awesome."

Elliot took a couple manila folders out of the box and then closed it.

"Ashley is clean as a whistle," he said, impatiently tossing her file aside. "But I'm pretty sure Lance has been cheating on his history tests."

"How can you tell?"

"Because *I've* been cheating on the tests, too," he said. "I went through everyone's files. Nobody's getting 100s, not even Ashley. And Lance is getting 110s! In every exam, Mr. Douglas includes two bonus questions about current events. I always skip them, to avoid suspicion. But Lance has been stupidly answering them, week after week. Last week, he answered a question about the Rwandan genocide. He's *clearly* cheating."

"How?"

"The same way I am," Elliot said. "By breaking into Douglas's desk each Tuesday night and copying down the answer key."

Even though I had known Elliot for some time now, I was still surprised by how casually he had confessed to cheating.

"Maybe he's just really good at history?" I said. "And, you know, follows the news about Rwanda?"

Elliot smiled.

"We'll find out."

• • •

I was always amazed by Elliot's knowledge. Not just the things he *knew,* but the things he *didn't* know. For instance: Elliot could recite the biography of every Roman emperor in history, from the number of palaces they built for themselves to the number of dwarfs they owned to the type of daggers they were murdered with. But he didn't know anything about the New York Mets, not even which league they were in.

He could recite Shakespeare's *Othello* from memory—or at least, all of Iago's monologues. But whenever I quoted *The Simpsons,* he looked at me with confusion and disgust, like I had broken into some kind of animal language of grunts and squeaks.

He knew how to trade commodities on the Japanese stock market and detect Michelangelo forgeries. But he couldn't make a paper airplane to save his life, and he had never even tried to toast a Pop-Tart.

He knew the functions of all of his father's companies—which ones made weapons, which ones made chemicals, and which ones made both. He knew the addresses of all of his father's homes and the number of servants assigned to each of them. He knew the thread count of his father's suits and the metric dimensions of his indoor Jacuzzi. But he didn't know his birthday.

And even though he knew my allergies, my shoe size, my locker combination, and God knows what else, he never seemed to know what I was thinking or feeling. Or why.

• • •

I was sitting next to Lance in science when Mr. Douglas marched into our class. He was one of our most laid-back teachers, a former Peace Corps member who played the same three Cat Stevens songs on guitar at every talent show. I had never seen him angry before, but now he looked furious. His face was flushed a fiery red and his ponytail had come unraveled. I wondered what a history teacher was doing in science class. He opened and closed his mouth a few times, but he was too angry to produce any sound.

"Lance," he managed, finally.

Lance stood up and started to unbutton his lab coat, but Mr. Douglas flicked his wrist impatiently.

"Just come," he said. *"Now."*

I excused myself to go to the bathroom and quietly followed them down the hall, toward the school's administrative wing.

The principal's door was glass, and when I walked by it, I caught a glimpse of the havoc Elliot had wrought. Principal Higgins was reading Lance's latest history exam and shaking his head in disgust. Lance's parents had been called in for the meeting. They sat on either side of their son, staring at him in horrified amazement. Lance stared down at his lap, his face a mask of fear.

• • •

"What happened to Lance?" I asked, on the limo ride back to Elliot's. "Did you tell on him?"

"Give me some credit," Elliot said. "I'm not some tattling *child*."

"If you didn't tell, then how did he get caught?"

Elliot cracked each of his knuckles, one by one, basking in my curiosity.

"Anyone with good information can destroy an enemy," he said, finally. "But it takes a subtle genius to get an enemy to destroy himself."

He dropped some ice cubes into a glass and filled it to the brim with Scotch.

"No interruptions," he said.

• • •

Mr. Douglas had several eccentricities, the most famous of which was his obsession with saving paper. Instead of printing out forty-one tests each week, he wrote out a single copy in longhand and read the questions out loud. We wrote our answers on scrap paper, which he scavenged from the other classrooms' recycling bins.

Mr. Douglas always wrote out his tests on Wednesdays, while supervising study hall. They took him about fifteen minutes to write. When he was finished, he waved the test in the air, announced the topic, and deposited it into a locking desk drawer. If Lance was cheating—and Elliot was certain that he was—he *had* to be getting his answers from this drawer. No other copies of the test ever existed.

The lock was impregnable without tools, Elliot explained, but the desktop itself was light enough to pry open. All you had to do was ratchet it up with a strong ruler and the drawer's contents would be exposed. Elliot usually broke into the desk at lunchtime, while the teachers and students were packed into the cafeteria. Elliot's allergies required him to visit the nurse's office every day at noon, to take an antihistamine. And Mr. Douglas's classroom was conveniently located right next door.

"Do you actually have allergies?" I asked him.

"What do you think?" he said.

Elliot had assumed that Lance was stealing the test on Wednesday evenings. As captain of the basketball team, he was required to stay an extra fifteen minutes after practice to put away the cones and balls. By the time he left the gym each day, the halls would be deserted, giving him ample time to break into Douglas's desk. Of course, by raiding the desk *after* Elliot had already had a chance to tamper with the test, he opened himself to sabotage.

"Did you take away the answer key? So he couldn't cheat?"

Elliot shook his head.

"If I took away the answer key, Douglas would know someone had broken into his desk. I left an answer key, all right. Just not a particularly useful one."

After copying Douglas's test at lunchtime, Elliot went into the nurse's office and faked a massive allergy attack. James arrived promptly and took him home, where the two of them constructed a counterfeit exam for Lance to copy a few hours hence. James took great pains to replicate Douglas's looping cursive. They kept Mr. Douglas's questions intact, but they replaced the answers. When they were finished with the forgery, James drove Elliot back to school so he could plant it in Douglas's desk. While Lance practiced free throws in the gym, Elliot strolled through the empty halls and quietly sealed my political opponent's fate.

Elliot staked out Mr. Douglas's classroom for a while from the classroom across the hall. And sure enough, after about an hour, he saw Lance creep into the room and copy down the answers from Elliot's phony exam. After Lance fled, Elliot took back his fake and returned Mr. Douglas's original.

The next morning, when Mr. Douglas read out his questions during history class, Lance wrote down Elliot's answers, wholly convinced of their accuracy.

"He was like a man accidentally signing his own death warrant," he told me, "or mistakenly digging his own grave."

"So you put in wrong answers?" I asked.

"Not exactly," Elliot said. "Even if Lance had gotten a zero on the test, he wouldn't have received any disciplinary action. He could've just claimed not to have studied. Everyone is entitled to an off day, even proven scholars like Lance."

"So what did you do? How did you get him in trouble for cheating?"

"I didn't," Elliot said, handing me his modified exam. "I got him in trouble for something far worse."

1) Which fearsome terrorist organization sprung up in the
South during the 1860s?

The Underground Railroad

2) Who commanded this group of terrorists?

Harriet Tubman

3) Which 1863 decree is commonly referred to as "our
country's finest law"?

The Poll Tax

4) Which series of laws have since been debunked as an
unjust perversion of democracy?

The Emancipation Proclamation

On and on it went, each answer more damning than the last.

"Lance wasn't punished for cheating," Elliot explained. "He
was punished for his hateful belief system."

I pictured Lance, sitting with his parents in the principal's office, weighing his nightmarish options. He was either a thieving
plagiarist or a horrible racist. Either way, his presidential campaign was over.

Elliot snatched the fake exam out of my hands, held it out the
window, and ignited it with a cigar lighter.

"One down," he said. "One to go."

James opened the sunroof and the smoke filtered out of the
limo. He was talking on his cell phone, but the soundproof window was closed and I couldn't hear what he was saying.

"Where did your father find James?" I asked.

"It's a long story," he said. "One that you'll enjoy immensely."

He was about to launch into it when the limo pulled up to the curb in front of a nondescript granite building.

"What's this place?" I asked.

Elliot sighed.

"My father's club."

Terry staggered down the stone steps and shuffled over to the car, his face unusually red. James hopped out of the limo and opened the door for him, discreetly holding his elbow to keep him from falling.

"Seymour!" he said. "It's always a thrill to see you. How is everything?"

"Great, Mr. Allagash," I said. "Elliot's about to tell me a story, about how you found James?"

"How I found James? Please! I don't have the energy or patience to find anyone. *James* found *me*!"

Elliot finished his drink and turned his gaze toward the window.

"I'll tell you the whole business," Terry told me. "We wouldn't want this one to butcher it. I'll give it to you in the study—but no interruptions!"

•••

"Fifteen years ago, I was sifting through my mail at this very desk when I came across an unusual postcard. The glossy side featured a terrifying painting of a skull. The other, a short handwritten message.

" 'The Giants will win Game One.'

"I threw the postcard into a special drawer my lawyers make

me keep for death threats and forgot about it, until the following week, when another morbid postcard landed on my desk. This one featured two dancing skeletons—and predicted another victory for the Giants. I ignored this card, too—and the next one, and the next one. But after seven weeks of receiving these mysterious cards, with their morbid illustrations and scribbled football predictions, I started to pay them some mind. You see, every single one of them had come true.

"When I received the eighth postcard—which predicted the Giants would lose to the subpar Eagles—I decided to take the anonymous kook at his word. I called up a friend from my club and placed a bet on Philadelphia. The postcard was correct, as usual, and I won a sizable sum. I continued to take my personal prophet's advice, betting more money each week as my confidence in his accuracy grew. By week twelve, I had made an amount of money so obscene that it was difficult to collect it without laughing.

"Who was sending the postcards? How did he track me down? Why was he giving me football predictions? What the hell was in it for him? I found out when the thirteenth postcard arrived in the mail.

" 'The trial period is over,' it said. 'Now that you've seen what I can do, why not subscribe to my service?' All I had to do was mail a thousand dollars to a PO box in Poughkeepsie, it promised, and a thirteenth prediction would arrive in the mail, 'by rush delivery,' just in time for Sunday's matchup against the Redskins.

"I called Duffy, an old Harvard friend who gambles full-time in Monte Carlo, and told him the entire story. At this point, my

theory was that my prophet was an NFL coach or referee, someone with inside information who couldn't risk placing the bets
himself. Duffy nixed that hypothesis in a hurry.

" 'He'd get in just as much hot water for mailing the postcards,'
he said. 'Giving information to gamblers is as illegal as gambling
itself. And besides, no ref would risk his job for a measly thousand
dollars.'

" 'What if he's someone lower down,' I asked, 'who's too poor
to make any real bets himself? Like a locker-room janitor? He
knows some inside information, perhaps, but he doesn't have a
thousand dollars on hand. So he buys a ten-cent postcard, sells his
info to a billionaire and turns a profit without investing any capi-
tal?'

" 'That's not a bad theory,' Duffy said. 'Except for one thing:
Inside information is never that good.'

" 'What if the games are being fixed?'

" 'NFL games can't be fixed,' Duffy said. 'Believe me, I've tried.
There are just too many variables. There are seven referees, a
dozen coaches, over a hundred players. It's not like paying a boxer
to take a dive. I mean, sure, you can get the quarterback to throw
some interceptions. But even that only gets you so far.'

" 'What if the whole team is conspiring together?'

" 'Nobody's pulled off a team-wide conspiracy since the Black
Sox. And besides, your prophet picks the Giants to *win* sometimes. Are the Giants' opponents throwing games, too? There's no
way someone bought the entire league. I would have heard about
it.'

" 'All right,' I said. 'Maybe he's not affiliated with the league.

Maybe he's just a gambling expert who's really talented at making picks.'

" '*I'm* a gambling expert who's really talented at making picks. I've never cracked eighty percent, ever. If I hit sixty-five percent it's a great year.'

" 'So what are you telling me? Is he an actual prophet?'

" 'Maybe he's the Devil,' Duffy said. 'Who cares? Just give me that thirteenth pick!'

"At this point, the prophet had earned me so much money that I almost felt as if I owed him something. So, with low expectations, I mailed the money to the PO box. His pick arrived the next day, as promised, and lo and behold, it was a good one. I collected a staggering amount of money from my clubmates. I would have won more, but most of them were no longer willing to bet against me on the Giants.

"The prophet's next postcard asked for fifty thousand dollars.

" 'You've got to pay!' Duffy shouted, over and over again, for a solid hour. I hung up on him, eventually, and mulled over the situation in this study. I still didn't know who my prophet was or how he knew so much about football. But I knew this: He had no reason to give me bad information. After all, if he picked a loser, I might stop paying for picks. It was in his best interest to keep feeding me winners.

"Eventually, I decided to choose the most rational course: I sold the pick to Duffy for sixty thousand dollars. He wired me the cash immediately, and I sent fifty of it to Poughkeepsie. The postcard arrived within forty-eight hours. It depicted some kind of altar made out of bones and foretold a Giants victory. I went down to the club on Sunday morning, but I couldn't convince anyone to bet against me. I was pretty frustrated, until the unthinkable happened: The Giants lost. I waited for another postcard, but it never arrived.

"At this point, my curiosity had grown so extreme that it was interfering with my day-to-day life. I thought about the prophet constantly: who he was, how he operated, that sort of thing. So I dispatched one of my personal investigators to Poughkeepsie to stake out that post office and find him. It wasn't easy. Nobody touched the box for days. Or at least, no *customer* touched the box. We eventually learned that my prophet had somehow gotten himself employed at the post office as a janitor. He was the only one with access to the boxes from one to nine A.M.—and that's when he collected his mail. In the end, I had no choice but to call in a favor from a friend at the Federal Reserve. We sent the prophet a bushel of marked bills (with a request for more picks), tracked their distribution, and traced them back to his parents' house in the suburbs. When the surveillance photos arrived, I thought there had been some kind of mistake. My prophet was a scrawny seventeen-year-old with long hair and acne. Some kid named James.

"He was relatively easy to abduct, once we knew his identity, and my people managed to extract a full confession without excessive violence. It was an amazing thing to listen to.

"The boy's father sold high-end diamond-and-silver cuff links, and my name and address were listed in his Rolodex. That's where the boy found *all* his addresses. You see, I wasn't the only one receiving postcards! At the start of the football season, the boy had sent out predictions to all twenty thousand of his father's contacts. He told ten thousand people that their home team would lose and ten thousand people that their home team would win. The following week, he determined which people had received accurate predictions and sent them each a follow-up postcard. Again, he told half of them that their home team would win and half that their home team would lose. He continued to whittle down his list in this fashion, week after week, until Game Thirteen arrived. At that point, only twenty-two names remained. Twenty of them were sufficiently impressed to 'subscribe' to his service. And the following week, of the twelve gullible millionaires that remained, six agreed to pay him fifty grand for his take on Game Fifteen. He lost me that week, along with three others. But two names remained, and both agreed to pay a hundred thousand dollars for James's Game Sixteen 'prediction.' One of those predictions proved accurate. And so there was still one man left, some steel tycoon in Pittsburgh, whose faith remained intact. He'd already sent James a million dollars for the inside dirt on the Super Bowl.

"By the time I caught up with James, he had netted a fortune from his football scam. It was an expensive undertaking—all those stamps and letters—but he was able to fund it with the profits from other scams. He'd completed hundreds by that age, each one more daring than the last.

" 'Are you going to kill me?' he asked when I introduced myself at the end of his four-hour interrogation.

" 'Good heavens, no!' I said. 'I'm going to offer you a job!' "

• • •

I found Elliot just outside the study, reading a thick, old military book.

"Why'd you leave in the middle of the story?" I asked.

"I've heard it before," he said.

."It's pretty amazing that your dad hired that guy."

Elliot waved his hand dismissively.

"My family has always employed at least one full-time con man. Terry wasn't the first Allagash to think of it."

"Isn't it risky to hire criminals?"

"Not if you're the only one who knows about their crimes. If James ever tried to hurt the family, we could reveal his offenses to the authorities. It keeps him in check."

"Do you think he *wants* to hurt your family?"

"Probably not. We pay him an outrageous salary, plus expenses. And we give him one month's vacation every year, so he can travel the world and visit all the foreign whores he keeps on retainer."

He unscrewed his pen and began to underline a lengthy passage in his book.

"Elliot?" I asked. "Does your dad have any more stories like that?"

Elliot shut his book.

"Why don't you knock on his study door and find out?" he snapped. "He's probably waiting for you in the vestibule, cupping his ear to the door to hear your approach! Go ahead!"

He took a handkerchief out of his pocket and coughed into it violently, his tiny body shaking from the force. I considered patting him on the back, but eventually decided against it. After a while, his fit subsided and he leaned against the wall, exhausted.

"If you want to hear a good story," he wheezed. "You should hear my scheme to eliminate Ashley."

I felt a sudden pang of guilt. I didn't mind when Elliot plotted against Lance or the Winchester. But Ashley was a really nice girl. She always volunteered to make decorations for class dances, even though she usually didn't go to them. In seventh grade, Mr. Hendricks had paired us up for the annual gingerbread house art project, and we had spent a whole afternoon at her place, laughing at soap operas and eating our materials. We weren't exactly friends, but she had never called me Chunk-Style, even at the height of the nickname's popularity. One time, she caught me singing the song "Barbie Girl" on the way back to class from the water fountain. It was the verse that goes, *I'm a Barbie girl, in a Barbie world,* and I was pretty much singing it at full voice. She could have told someone about the incident, but she never did.

"You're not going to do anything really bad to her, are you?"

Elliot didn't seem to hear me. He dialed James.

"Maybe this isn't a good idea," I said, finally. "I mean, it's just class president. I don't really care that much if I win."

Elliot slammed the phone down and stared at me.

"If you think this is about something as petty as class president, you're an even greater fool than I imagined! This is just a stepping stone—a stepping stone to a stepping stone to *a stepping stone to a—*"

He stopped suddenly and forced an odd chuckle.

"Look," he said. "I couldn't care less what you do. This is just a game to me."

He shrugged his shoulders.

"You're probably right. Who wants to be *president*? I mean honestly, who has the patience to pose for all those damn pictures?"

"Yeah," I said. "Right?"

Elliot nodded.

"Right. And then there are all those stupid meetings with the student senate? And those ridiculous interviews with *The Glendale Gazette*!"

"Yeah . . . it's all kind of silly."

"It's beyond silly! Everyone sucking up to you all the time to try to get this or that! And Jessica and her idiotic dance committee! Can you imagine going over to her house to plan one of those abominations?"

"Uh . . ."

"Besides," he said, "your parents probably won't care if you lose the election. In fact, they might even be *expecting* you to lose."

He opened his book and continued to underline the passage from where he had left off.

"Of course," he added softly, "it might be an interesting experience."

I sat down next to him.

"What are you going to do to Ashley?"

Elliot shrugged.

"Something elegant."

"Is it mean?"

Elliot laughed.

"Is it 'mean' to take a bishop with a rook? Is it 'mean' to sink a bank shot with a bridge? This is politics!"

"Maybe you're right," I said.

"Of course I'm right," he said. "Now let's shoot some pool."

It didn't occur to me until after the election that I hadn't actually asked for any details about his plan. Somehow, at the time, I was able to convince myself that this was an oversight, that I had remained ignorant of Elliot's machinations simply by accident— that I didn't know what I was getting into.

• • •

"You know we still haven't met Elliot," my father said. "Why don't you invite him over for your birthday? His dad can come along too, if he's not too busy."

"I don't know," I said. "Elliot's kind of a picky eater."

"We'll figure something out," he said. "I can always grill burgers. Everybody likes burgers, right? Pass the ketchup."

I passed him the bottle and he squeezed it over his chicken. A trickle of red liquid sputtered out of the nozzle.

"Damn it," he said.

He turned the bottle upside down and waited for the ketchup to ooze downward.

"Maybe we should go out to dinner." my mom said. "We could go to the St. Regis, maybe, or Tavern on the Green? You know, someplace . . ."

My dad laughed.

"Someplace *what?*"

"Someplace . . . fun," my mom said. "I mean, it's a special occasion, right? Fourteen's a big age!"

My dad nodded.

"Then we'll bake a cake," he said.

• • •

My dad was an assistant professor of economics at Fordham. He sometimes wrote articles in journals, long essays with footnotes and diagrams and graphs. He had also written a book, which an agent had recently submitted to publishers. I was really proud of the fact that my father had written an entire book, and it wasn't until Elliot asked me to describe it that I realized I had no idea what it was about. "Something with Marx" was all I could manage.

"Oh," Elliot said. "One of those."

I winced. I didn't know that other people had written about this Marx guy before. I hoped my dad knew.

My mom worked afternoons as a speech therapist, but on the night of the Allagash dinner, she called in sick to concentrate on cooking. When I got home from school, there were so many kitchen appliances running at once, we had to shout to hear each other.

"Look on your desk!" she told me. "Dad and I got you a birthday present!"

I gave her a giant hug and sprinted breathlessly down the hall. I had asked for only one thing that year—NBA Slam '98—and I felt pretty good about my chances. My parents didn't like video games, but they had bought me NBA Slam '97 the previous year, and in my opinion that had set a pretty firm precedent. I unwrapped the package slowly, mentally rehearsing the look of surprise I would treat my mother to when the game was finally in my hands.

It was clothes. There was a brown belt, a dark-blue button-down shirt with a stiff collar, and a strange pair of brown shoes that didn't have any laces. I rooted around in the package for a while, in the hope that my mother had hidden the game beneath the clothes as some kind of practical joke. Eventually I gave up and shouted out as cheerful a thank-you as I could muster.

I changed into my favorite Knicks jersey and went to the kitchen to dull my pain with some Yoo-hoos. When I passed my mom, she had a panicked expression on her face.

"Aren't you going to try on your new clothes?" she asked.

It took me a few attempts to get the shirt to button evenly, but I eventually figured it out. By the time I went back out for my second Yoo-hoo, my parents were arguing about something.

"No," my dad was saying. "This was the one we were saving. The one from Italy."

"Are you sure?" my mom asked. "I thought we were saving the other bottle?"

My dad laughed.

"It doesn't matter," he said. "You already opened it."

He looked at me—and then back at my mother.

"Are those new clothes?" he asked.

• • •

There was a movie that came out when I was little called *The Jetsons Meet the Flintstones*. In the movie, the two families get along almost immediately and end up working together to save the world. Maybe it was the fact that I had seen this movie so many times that made me so optimistic about our dinner with the Allagashes.

Elliot and Terry entered in bowler hats. It clearly threw my father, but he recovered quickly and thrust out his hand.

"Thanks for coming," he said. "I'm so glad you could make it."

"It's a pleasure to finally meet you!" Terry said.

He took off his coat and peered across the living room, craning his neck slightly. It took him a fairly long time to realize that no servant was going to take his coat and briefcase. Eventually, he draped them awkwardly over a chair. The grown-ups started talking about the weather and Elliot and I went into my bedroom.

"What kind of rodent is that?" Elliot asked, gesturing at my pet mouse.

"It's a mouse," I said. "His name's Houdini. I've been trying to train him to stand and he's almost got it."

"Show me."

I held a food pellet over his head and shouted "Up!" a few times. Eventually, after some deliberation, Houdini struggled onto his hind legs and grabbed it with his paws. I rubbed his neck and fed him an extra pellet as a reward.

"Not bad," Elliot said.

"Do you have any pets?" I asked.

Elliot stared at me for a moment.

"Not exactly," he said.

• • •

"I'm so glad you liked the cake," my mother said.

"It's *superb*," Terry said. "It's a good thing I left room for dessert!"

"I'm sorry you're not big on hamburgers," my father said to Elliot. "You still hungry? There's a slice of brisket in the fridge, if you don't mind leftovers."

Elliot stared confusedly at my father.

"Left . . . overs?"

There was a long pause. Eventually, Terry cleared his throat and smiled at my father.

"Elliot tells me you've written a book," he said. "Congratulations!"

My dad laughed awkwardly.

"It's being shopped around," he said. "It could easily end up in a drawer."

"He's being modest," my mom said. "There's some real interest from two different university presses. One in St. Louis and another one in Canada."

My father sighed.

"That's wonderful," Terry said. "I have some friends in publishing. Are you familiar with Bishop House?"

"Yes," my father said. "In fact, they were one of the first houses to reject me."

"They said it was too 'academic,' " my mom explained.

"Actually, I think the word they used was 'boring,' " my dad said. "But hey, same difference. Are you sure you don't want any of this wine, Terry? It's a pretty good Italian one."

"No, thank you," he said.

My father poured himself another glass. I noticed that he was the only one drinking.

My mother stared anxiously at Elliot's untouched slice of cake. When it became clear he wasn't going to try it, she poured out a large glass of milk and placed it hopefully beside his bony hand.

"So Elliot," she said, "I hear you're quite the basketball player! I can't believe how much the two of you have been practicing. You must really love it!"

I shot Elliot a desperate look and he sighed wearily.

"Yes," he deadpanned. "My favorite sport is basketball."

"Well, that's great!" my mother said. "That's just great."

She topped off his milk, even though he hadn't yet drunk any.

"Between *basketball* and the *asbestos club* and *being Seymour's campaign manager*, I don't know how you have time for all your homework! How many extracurricular activities are you involved in?"

"Many," he said.

My father held his wine glass to the light and rotated it slightly, squinting at the sediment that had collected in the bottom.

"Are you a wine drinker?" he asked Terry.

"Yes," Terry said. "I actually went to a tasting earlier this afternoon. If it hadn't been so comprehensive, I gladly would have joined you in a toast. But I'm afraid I'm just not up to it at this stage in the evening."

My father nodded and looked across the table at my mother.

"I usually only have wine on special occasions," he said. "For example, one of my colleagues brought me back a bottle of wine from his parent's village in Italy. I was going to save it for the day

I sold my book. But now I realize, hey, what if I don't sell it at all? A failed book is no reason to waste wine, right?"

Terry cleared his throat.

"My goodness, Seymour," he said. "I forgot to give you your present!"

He stood up and pulled a package out of his large briefcase. It was wrapped in reflective silver paper and tied with thick gold ribbon.

"Oh, you *shouldn't* have!" my mom cried.

The gift wrap was so elaborate that it took me a while to tear through it all. When I was finally finished and the gift lay exposed on the table, a hush settled over the room. It was a brand-new Sega Dreamcast video-game *system.*

I had read articles in video game magazines announcing its arrival, but I had never actually beheld one. It was a beautiful machine, sleek and silver. When I lifted it out of the box, I let loose an involuntary shriek; there were more than a dozen games hidden beneath it.

"Oh my God," I said. "Oh my God."

I realized that I was standing up. I composed myself, sat back down, and thanked Mr. Allagash profusely.

"You *really* shouldn't have," my mother repeated.

Terry waved his hands.

"It's my pleasure!"

"No," my father said. "Really. You shouldn't have."

I brought the gift into my bedroom and a short, handwritten note fell out of the box. It was hidden beneath the mountain of games and I hadn't initially noticed it.

Dear Seymour,

Thank you for spending so much time with my strange, strange boy. What is it like? You must remind me to ask you sometime.

   Terry

I put the bizarre note in my desk drawer and went back out to join the party. But by the time I got there, it had broken up. Everyone was standing around by the front door—except for my father, who was still at the table, finishing his wine and staring at my pile of crumpled gift wrapping.

"Are you sure you don't want to stay and play a game?" my mother asked. "Charades? Pictionary?"

"Oh, I don't know," Terry said. "It's getting late."

He started to put on his coat.

"We've also got Uno and Boggle?"

"Thanks for offering," he said. "But I think we're just too tired."

My father set his glass down, loudly.

"How about Monopoly," he said.

Terry stopped in his tracks.

"Did you say Monopoly?"

• • •

Terry and Elliot sat on one side of the board, facing my father. My mother and I had gone completely bankrupt within the first thirty minutes of the game. That left just my father and the Allagashes, who had elected to play as a team.

"Bedtime is ten o'clock," my mother said. "So I guess whoever's winning in five minutes wins!"

"That sounds reasonable," Terry said.

"No three, four, or six," my dad muttered, cradling the dice in his palm. *"No three, four, or six."*

He shook the dice some more, clearly stalling. The Allagashes had set up hotels on all three orange properties, and he was just one bad roll away from bankruptcy.

"You know, it's not too late to accept our trade," Terry told him. "Thirteen hundred dollars is quite a generous sum for Pennsylvania Avenue."

"Actually, our offer was *twelve* hundred," Elliot corrected. "But still, an excellent deal."

My father put down the dice and glared at them.

"I already told you," he said. "I'm not giving up my monopoly. Not for any amount of money."

Terry chuckled.

"Suit yourself."

There seemed to be a lot riding on this game. Usually, if I offered my dad a trade, he would accept it automatically. But when I offered him a get-out-of-jail-free card for Short Line Railroad, he had flatly rejected me. My father rolled the dice and I held my breath as they skittered across the board. They collided with some Allagash hotels and eventually came to a stop by the Community Chest cards: a three . . . and a four.

"Seven!" I shouted. "That's Free Parking!"

My father thrust his fist in the air and made a grunting noise.

"Yes!" he shouted. "Yes!"

I held up my hand and he slapped it, hard.

"What time is it?" I asked. "Is it ten, Mom?"

"Um . . ."

"It's ten!" my father said, waving his watch in the air. "It's exactly ten! Game over!"

He leaned forward and scooped up the enormous stack of money from the center of the board, while laughing and tousling my hair.

"Congratulations," Terry said, extending his hand.

My father slapped it.

"Don't feel too bad for losing, Terry. I'm an economics professor, so this game is kind of my thing."

"You know," Elliot said. "Strictly speaking Free Parking isn't an official part of the—"

Terry cut him off.

"Thanks for having us," he said. "We had a wonderful time."

• • •

My father leaned back in his chair while my mother finished Windexing the table.

"Did you see the look on Terry's face?" he said. "When I rolled that seven?"

My mother scooped some crumbs into her cupped hand and went back into the kitchen without responding.

"It was great, Dad," I said. "Really, really great."

"You'd think a business tycoon would know a little something about Monopoly! Especially a robber baron like Terry Allagash! Oh man . . . that family hasn't been creamed like that since the Sherman Act!"

I had no idea what he was talking about, but I laughed along anyway. It was the happiest I'd seen him since he'd handed in his book six weeks earlier.

"The trick is to *control the board,*" he said. "I knew I had them in the palm of my hand with those greens so I—"

The phone rang. He answered with a cheery "Hey!"—but his smile quickly faded.

"Yes . . . okay . . . I understand . . ."

He took the phone into his bedroom and closed the door. My mother, who had been watching from the kitchen, sat down next to me.

"What's going on?" I asked her.

She didn't respond. She just kept her eyes locked on the closed door. Eventually, my father came out and slumped down beside us. His face was pale. He didn't say anything.

"What's wrong?" my mom whispered. "Who was that?"

"My agent," he said. "They sold my book."

"Oh my gosh!" my mom shouted, throwing her arms around his neck. "I'm so proud of you! Oh, we need to celebrate!"

She poured the last bit of wine into a glass and handed it to my father.

"Which one was it? The St. Louis one?"

"No."

"The Canadian one?"

"No."

"Then . . . who was it?"

"It was Bishop," he said, forcing a smile. "They changed their minds. In the middle of the night."

He stared at the wine glass for a moment and handed it back to my mother.

"Cheers," he said.

• • •

My parents usually policed my television watching, but they were having some kind of argument in their bedroom and didn't have time to deal with me. I sat on the living room couch for hours, watching old sitcoms, trying to make out their distant voices. Eventually, they came out of the bedroom and sat on either side of me. I apologized for watching TV so late, but I could tell they weren't mad. My mom unbuttoned my shirt collar and rubbed my neck.

"I'm sorry the shirt was so itchy," she said.

"It's okay," I said.

"You don't have to wear it again," she said.

My dad turned off the television, grabbed me a glass of water from the kitchen and sat back down next to me.

"Dad?" I asked. "Are they going to make your book?"

My parents shared a look.

"Yeah," my dad said, finally. "They sure are."

I hugged him.

"Wow, first Monopoly and now this!"

My dad laughed.

"Anyone can land on Free Parking," he said. "But thanks, kiddo."

My mom brought me my retainer and the two of them tucked me into bed, making sure to turn on the bathroom light on their way out.

I was heading into a deep sleep when the phone rang out violently in every room in the apartment. I knew it was Elliot calling (who else could it be?) and that the ringing would wake up my parents. But I was too groggy to answer it immediately. By the time I crawled across the bed and grabbed the receiver, my mother was on the other line. She sounded disoriented. I don't think anybody had ever called the house that late.

"It's okay, Mom," I said. "I got it."

"Good night," she murmured. "Good night, sweetie."

As soon as she hung up, Elliot launched into a monologue. He was speaking so fast that at first it was difficult to understand him.

"Elliot, I'm sorry," I said. "I can't talk about the election right now."

"This isn't about the election," he said. "It's a completely new scheme. When I was sabotaging Douglas, I figured out a way to crack his final exam."

"Why do you need to cheat on that, Elliot? You're *good* at history. You're always reading those books about wars and stuff."

"Right—*that's* history. Not Douglas's parade of namby-pamby socialist fairy tales! I refuse to devote even one second of mental effort to figuring out which myth he wants me to invoke! The melting pot? Susan B. Anthony? Sacagawea? *Sacagawea?* She was a servant girl!"

"What?"

"Listen to me. *If Douglas thinks—*"

"Elliot, can you tell me about all this tomorrow? I'm kind of tired."

He kept on talking. Loud classical music was playing in the background and his voice was slightly slurred.

"It's so obvious!" he shouted. "Mr. Douglas writes his major exams over the weekend, so there's no way to steal it from his desk. But if some higher authority demanded to see the exam in advance, Douglas would have no choice but to submit it! I know what you're thinking: Which authority, right?"

"Elliot . . ."

"A *fake* one! I have James impersonate the head of a scholastic awards organization. He writes Mr. Douglas a letter on gilded stationary, with a wax seal. 'Dear Mr. Douglas: We've been aware of your exam-writing talents for some time and would like to consider you for the prestigious Gladys Violet Award . . . ' "

"Elliot, listen . . ."

"James asks him to send in his upcoming history final as a sample of his work. I memorize the answers, get a perfect score—and here's the kicker! I write my test in purple ink! Get it? Gladys *Violet*? Purple? He'll know I orchestrated everything! Of course, he'll have no way to prove anything and even if he *could* he would be far too mortified to confront me. He might even convince himself that it was a coincidence and that he really had been nominated for some kind of teaching award. But deep down, the shame would fester in his heart, growing with every passing year, gnawing at his ego, driving him to the brink of madness—"

"Elliot, listen, it's late. I need to go to sleep."

"Absolutely not. We have work to do."

"I'm really tired."

"Trust me, you'll want to witness this! Go downstairs. James will pick you up in five minutes, and you'll stay the night."

"I have to wake up early tomorrow. My dad's making waffles."

"You don't like waffles. If you come here, James will make you a pie for breakfast, one of those disgusting ones you like so much, with the layer of sugar on top."

"I really can't. But hey, I promise I'll come over tomorrow, as soon as I can."

"Good Lord, I don't actually *care* whether you come or not! Jesus! I just don't understand why you would choose a food you dislike over a food you like."

"It's Sunday and my dad always makes waffles, and we serve them to my mom in bed. It's kind of like a tradition, because—"

"Great, whatever! I don't care!"

"Okay, well I'll see you tomorrow, Elliot. Elliot? You still there?"

• • •

I was rushing out of French class—it was Taco Day in the cafeteria—when Mr. Hendricks tapped me on the shoulder.

"Seymour," he said, "is it all right if I talk to you for a moment?"

He must have sensed my nervousness, because he quickly added, "Don't worry, you're not in trouble."

I sighed with relief and followed him back into his empty classroom.

"How's the club going?" he asked.

"The what?"

"The . . . Anti-Asbestos League?"

"Oh!" I said. "It's going great."

He nodded enthusiastically.

"That's great," he said. "And how's the campaign going? I notice you haven't put up any posters."

I nodded.

"Elliot's the campaign manager," I said. "So that stuff's pretty much his call."

Mr. Hendricks nodded.

"Ashley's sure put up a lot of posters, huh?" he said.

"Yeah," I said. "They're really neat."

"She's *super* excited about the campaign. I don't know if you know this, but I'm going to be the council's faculty advisor next year."

"Congratulations."

"I know!" he said. "It's exciting, right? Anyway, Ashley has already sent me *five* proposals! For bake sales and dances and charity walks. Isn't that amazing?"

I nodded slowly, unsure of what he was getting at.

"Anyway," he said, "the reason I wanted to talk to you is that I actually had a little brainstorm recently, and I wanted to run it by you. This morning, I was walking through the park, and I thought to myself: Hey, wait a minute—we have two exceptional candidates who are passionate about public service . . . why not have them work together? We wouldn't have to bother with any speeches or posters. We could just call this election business off and have co-presidents! What do you think?"

"That sounds pretty good," I said. "I'll talk to Elliot and see what he thinks."

Mr. Hendricks craned his neck to see if anyone was standing in the doorway. Then he leaned in close and continued in a low voice.

"Listen, Seymour," he said. "I'm only telling you this because I think you're mature enough to keep it between us. But Ashley's been having a pretty rough year."

"What do you mean?"

"You know how you and Elliot have the Anti-Asbestos League? And Lance has the basketball team? She doesn't really have anything like that. If she doesn't get to do this, I think she'll be pretty upset. I haven't run this co-presidents idea by her yet, but I think if *you* suggested it to her, she'd be very excited. I think *everybody* would."

I nodded. My parents would still be proud of me if I was co-president and I'd still get to be in the yearbook. Besides, I didn't really know how to be president anyway. It would be way easier to do it with Ashley than by myself—and probably more fun. We could organize another gingerbread house contest; if we named ourselves judges, we'd have free rein over the supplies.

"So you'll think about it?"

"Sure," I said.

"Oh, that's great news!"

"Although . . . I really need to talk to Elliot first."

Mr. Hendricks sighed.

"Of course."

• • •

Elliot finished his martini and wheeled his glass down the dumb-waiter for a refill.

"Do you know what 'co-president' is in a two-way race?" he asked me.

"What?"

"Dead last."

He fired a breaking shot and paced around the billiards table a few times, stopping only to snatch his new drink.

"I think it might be a good idea," I said. "I mean, I'd still get to be president. But I wouldn't have to hurt Ashley's feelings, or risk losing."

Elliot banged his tiny fist against the table. The impact was barely audible against the green felt.

"If I'm managing your campaign," he said, "it's *not* a *risk!*"

He handed me his drink as he hunched over for his next shot. His glass was practically overflowing, and I instinctively sipped at it to avoid a spill. The taste was shocking—like a cloud of misfired bug spray—and it set off a lengthy coughing fit.

"Don't you realize what's going on here?" Elliot said. "Mr. Hendricks is *scared* of you. He's afraid you're going to defeat Ashley! You're *winning,* Seymour, and we haven't even done anything yet!"

He lined up a long shot.

"Mr. Hendricks thinks you're some kind of rube. I can't wait to see his face when you're president of the entire grade!"

I remembered how disappointed Ashley had looked at the last election, holding back tears and comforting Han Wo, the foreign exchange student who was her only ally. But then I imagined the principal announcing my name, on stage, in front of everyone. I pictured myself posing alone for the yearbook picture, wearing the new suit my parents had bought me now that I was too thin for the old one.

"I guess it would be pretty cool," I said.

I took a second sip of Elliot's drink. It was as horrible as the first sip, but I managed not to cough this time.

"What was Mr. Hendricks wearing when he pulled you aside?" Elliot asked. "Let me guess: that plaid number, with the wooden buttons."

"Yeah," I said. "How'd you know?"

"Well, the man only has two jackets," he said. "And he wore the brown one yesterday. So . . ."

"Basic reasoning."

"Exactly!"

Elliot knocked in his shot and reached for some chalk. I started to hand him his drink back, but he waved it off.

"Keep it," he said. "I'll get another."

"So should we get started on that speech?" I asked.

"Stop by tomorrow," he said. "I have some things to take care of first."

• • •

"Seymour, what a pleasant surprise. Elliot's gone for a drive with James. No need to leave, though—he'll be back within the hour.

Why don't you sit down over there, by my bear? I have an amusing and lengthy story that you must hear at once. No interruptions.

"Do you see this idiotic figurine? It's my proudest possession: Harvard Chess Champion, 1954. I've never been a very good chess player, you see, but I was *always* a talented cheater. This trophy proves it.

"I'll never forget the day I first laid eyes upon the Chess Ladder in the Harvard dining hall. It was a beautiful thing: a slab of solid mahogany, studded with golden name plaques. By challenging and defeating your superiors, you could gradually climb your way up the board. It was a yearlong free-for-all, and whoever held the top spot by graduation would be crowned the champion of his class.

"When I scanned the names on the ladder, I realized that I didn't recognize a single one of them. None of them had gone to Exeter or Andover or joined any of the social clubs I frequented. Some of the names were actually *foreign* sounding. It was a total meritocracy, and for the first time in my life, I felt excluded.

"I had never played chess before, and I had no interest in the game. But as soon as I saw that board, I resolved to dominate it.

"My first step was to enlist a chess expert to help me cheat. I found one at MIT, a nervous young man named Fishman who had topped his own school's chess ladder for years. He had student loans to pay, so it was easy to acquire his services.

"For the first five matches, we used a simple sign-language scheme. When my opponent and I sat down, Fishman and his roommate set up their own game at a nearby table. When my opponent made a move, I communicated it to Fishman with a series of signals designed to mimic mental exertion—sighs, head scratches, curses, etc. Fishman, in turn, would signal the correct move back to me using the same code. The signals we used ensured that Fishman would look engrossed in his own game, when in fact he was engrossed in mine. Our system was occasionally conspicuous. During one match, my opponent moved his rook across the entire length of the board, and I had to say the word 'cocksucker' eight consecutive times, loudly: 'Cocksucker, cocksucker, cocksucker, cocksucker, cocksucker, cocksucker, cocksucker, cocksucker.'

"My opponent was taken aback, but all chess players have their eccentricities, and he didn't comment on it. I always stayed composed during the matches, but the strain on poor Fishman was intense. I was paying him an incredible amount of money per victory—I'd say the equivalent of a Rhodes scholarship—and by the end of each contest he was drenched in sweat.

"As I made my way up the Chess Ladder, it became increasingly difficult to cheat. Upper-tier matches took place within the confines of the Harvard Chess Club—so that only members could observe the games in person—and Fishman wasn't a member. I was able to sneak him into the bathroom, but I could only make so many trips to the toilet before people started to get suspicious. We experimented with concealed two-way radios—at the time a new technology. But that required me to give a kind of running commentary into my lapel.

" 'Ah,' I'd say, leaning toward my bug-sized microphone. 'I see you've taken my rook with your bishop. Not the rook on the left, which was near the queen, but that other rook.'

"Chess players are not naturally confrontational. But by the time I entered the number five spot, my opponents were growing bolder.

" 'We know you're cheating,' they'd say. Or, 'You're obviously cheating.' Or, 'Please, Terry, why won't you stop cheating?'

"But they couldn't prove anything, and the matches continued. By the final week of classes, I had only one man to unseat to become champion. He was one of those adorable communists from Russia, a scrawny, bearded creature with wild, beady eyes. I don't remember his name.

"There were several obstacles in my path. By this point, the chess community was watching me so closely that none of my old strategies proved usable. The communist would only accept my challenge if I submitted to a variety of humiliating terms, designed to thwart my schemes. We were to play in an empty tent, which the communist would provide, and no audience would be admitted. I was to be strip-searched prior to the match for crib notes and electronic devices. And if I left the tent during the match, for any reason, I would forfeit automatically.

"I was still fairly confident that I would find a way. I met with Fishman in our usual spot, on a bench halfway down the Charles River. I paid him for the previous match and told him about the next one. The meeting was proceeding well enough until I casually mentioned the name of my final opponent.

" 'You're playing *who?*' he asked, his stammer even more pronounced than usual.

"I repeated the name.

"Fishman stared blankly at the water. His cheap oxford shirt, I noticed, was already mottled with a couple damp splotches.

" 'You mean . . . you've never heard of him?' he asked.

" 'Of course not,' I said. 'He's a chess player.'

"Fishman began to tell me about the man's 'career' in low, reverent tones. You see, even though the communist considered himself a revolutionary, he had apparently devoted most of his life to mastering this child's game. Consequently, he was very skilled at it.

" 'I've studied his matches,' Fishman said. 'When he won the world tournament in Zurich, the International Chess League named a variation after him. He was only fifteen.'

"He stared off into the distance.

" 'I'm sorry,' he said. 'I can't help you.'

" 'That's all right,' I said. 'Who do you recommend I hire in your place?'

"He laughed incredulously.

" 'Don't you get it?' he said. 'He's the best there is. It doesn't matter who you hire. You're definitely going to lose.'

"I met with the communist the following morning in his decrepit off-campus apartment. He was hosting some kind of meeting, and when I opened the door, he was in the middle of a high-pitched rant.

" 'I'll let you continue your rant in a moment,' I said. 'But first I'd like to discuss your terms.'

"The communist rolled his eyes and muttered something to his comrades, who were among the dirtiest men I'd ever seen.

" 'They're good terms,' I said, taking care not to touch anything in the room. 'And I'll agree to all of them—on *two* conditions. First, I would like to postpone the match for one week."

" 'What for?' he scoffed.

" 'To study,' I said. 'I only started playing this game about a month ago. It's all still pretty new to me.'

"He swallowed bitterly.

" 'What is your other term?' he grumbled.

" 'You must agree to the same conditions as I have,' I said. 'If I am searched, *you* must be searched. If I cannot leave the tent, *you* cannot leave the tent.'

"The communist threw back his head and laughed.

" 'You honestly believe that I would cheat against someone like you?'

"I smiled at the communists and shrugged.

" 'What can I say? I've always been a believer in fairness."

"I shook hands with my opponent, rinsed off my hands in a nearby fountain, and headed back to my club. The elderly steward handed me my usual afternoon drink, but I declined. He examined the glass to make sure he had mixed it correctly, and when he saw that he had, he immediately asked me if I was ill.

" 'I'm fine, Claverly,' I said. 'I'm just preparing for an important chess match.'

" 'Is there anything I can bring you?' he asked.

" 'Yes, actually,' I said. 'Some books.'

" 'On chess?'

" 'No,' I said. 'On nutrition.'

"A small crowd assembled at Harvard Yard on the morning of the match. They were mostly chess club members, but there were a few regular humans as well, including a reporter and photographer from the student newspaper. The communist and I posed for a picture in front of the tent and then followed the chess club president into a nearby bathroom, so he could search us for contrivances.

" 'Have you lost weight?' he asked me when I removed my shirt.

"I shrugged.

" 'Studying too hard, perhaps,' I said.

"After peering into our ears and searching our bodies for wires, he led us back out into the sun, to Harvard Yard, where the tent had been erected. It was empty, as promised, except for a table and a board.

" 'Can we request some coffee?' I asked the communist. 'Or does that go against your terms?'

"The communist hesitated.

" 'Fine,' he said. 'Coffee.'

"The club president brought us two thermoses of coffee and placed them on the table, next to the championship figurine. Then he closed the flaps of the tent.

"The communist made the first move—something with the knight, I think. I leaned back, folded my arms and smiled at him.

"Ten minutes passed.

" 'Quit stalling,' he said.

" 'This isn't speed chess,' I told him. 'I'll take as long as I want.'

"Another ten minutes passed.

" 'You're only delaying the inevitable,' he said. 'Make your move.'

"I smiled at the communist and leaned in close.

" 'Oh, I *am* making my move,' I whispered. 'I'm making it as we speak.'

"His beady eyes darted around the tent.

" 'What are you talking about?'

"I raised my coffee thermos and poured it out, slowly, onto the grass.

" 'Whoever leaves the tent, for any reason, forfeits the match.'

" 'So?'

" '*So,* I've subsisted on a protein diet for the past four days. I haven't consumed a diuretic in a week and I've avoided liquids and solids of all kinds for thirty-six hours. *You* just polished off an entire thermos of coffee.'

"His bushy brown eyebrows crinkled with anger and shock.

" 'You're crazy,' he said. 'You're a crazy person.'

"I leaned back in my chair.

" 'We'll see about that,' I said.

"Twelve hours later, I moved a random pawn and he took it with his knight. Then four more hours passed.

"The communist tried his best to remain composed, but he was obviously experiencing serious physical difficulties. Every few minutes, he clenched his fist and grimaced for a few seconds. These grimaces, I noticed, were coming at shorter and shorter intervals.

" 'You're a bastard,' he said. 'A bastard from hell.'

" 'I thought communists didn't believe in hell,' I said.

" 'Okay,' he muttered. 'I'll offer you a technical draw.'

"His legs, I noticed, were firmly crossed.

" 'Why would I accept?' I said. 'I'm winning.'

"A few beads of sweat slid slowly down his forehead. I could tell that he was weighing his options. Theoretically, he could relieve himself inside the tent. But what about his dignity? He was still a human being, after all, communist or not.

"At the twenty-two-hour mark, after flashing me one final look of disgust, he dashed out of the tent, his hands already fumbling with his cheap brown belt. I strolled out seconds later, trophy in hand. It was the proudest moment of my college career. Somehow, I had used my reputation as a cheater to help me commit the dirtiest cheat in the history of chess!

"All the spectators had left the yard except for the chess club president, whose face was flushed with anger.

" 'We're going to put an asterisk next to your name,' he informed me.

" 'You better,' I said.

"He snorted with contempt.

" 'So you won the trophy,' he said. '*So what?* What good is a trophy if it stands for nothing?'

"I laughed.

" 'For nothing? Good God, man, have some perspective! There are more important games in this world than *chess.*' "

• • •

"Yes, I know, I've heard it a million times. Protein diet. Very clever."

"You don't like that story?"

"What's impressive about it?" Elliot said. "It's vulgar on almost every possible level."

It was the day of the election. James had picked me up on the way to school so we could discuss my speech—which Elliot still hadn't told me anything about.

"There's a rumor that Ashley has some kind of surprise for the end of her speech," I said. "What do you think it is?"

"Don't worry about her speech," Elliot said. "Just focus on memorizing your own."

He handed me a small slip of paper. There couldn't have been more than fifty words typed on it.

"What's this? At the end?"

"It's a chant," Elliot said. "Just repeat it over and over again, and everyone will join in."

"Are you sure that'll work?"

Elliot nodded.

"Chanting is the most effective tool for controlling the masses. Along with propaganda."

"Where'd you learn that?"

"Don't worry about it," he said.

He handed me a Glendale hat, emblazoned with a lion, the school's official mascot.

"When you're called up to the podium, put this on," he said. "But *don't* put it on until you're about to start chanting."

The limo pulled up to the school.

"That's it?" I asked.

Elliot nodded.

"That's it."

• • •

Elliot had vowed to "eliminate Ashley," but on the morning of the election, she was still very much in the race. The hallways were lined with her tidy yellow flyers, touting her "Effort, Energy, and Efficiency." She had handed out buttons a few days before the election, and when I shuffled into the auditorium I noticed that a few kids were wearing them.

"I could easily get her disqualified before the race," Elliot had explained. "But winning by forfeit is exactly the same as losing. A victory has no meaning unless you've defeated someone, and defeated them harshly."

I understood his logic. But I still didn't see how I could defeat Ashley, no matter how well written Elliot's speech was.

My confidence waned even more when her name was called and she marched to the podium looking cautiously confident in a grown-up pantsuit. Her speech was loaded with facts and statistics and all sorts of big words. She was trying to make eye contact with as many people as possible and it made her French braid swing behind her, like a pendulum.

"If we increase the number of bake sales by twenty percent," she said, "and reallocate our funds, we could vastly increase the number of recreational events."

Most of her speech was hard for me to follow, since I knew nothing about student government. But my ears perked up when she got to the end.

"There's a rumor going around that I've planned a surprise for you all today. That rumor is true! In past years, lots of candidates have promised you a scoreboard. I always thought this was a really fun idea, and I'm super excited to announce that with the help of Mr. Hendricks and the generosity of Shamba Electronics, I was able to get us one!"

A bald electrician in a green jumpsuit walked through the side door.

"Sorry I'm late," he whispered from the edge of the stage.

"It's okay," Ashley said. "You made it just in time."

Ashley had been checking her watch repeatedly throughout the speech. I had assumed it was to make sure she didn't exceed the five-minute time limit. Really, though, she had been waiting for her scoreboard to arrive. I couldn't help but feel betrayed. I didn't care if Mr. Hendricks was rooting for Ashley, but he didn't have to help her find a *scoreboard.*

The electrician wheeled a large black slab draped with a white sheet on stage and everyone burst into applause. The teachers tried to conceal their excitement, out of fairness, but within seconds they were clapping too, and I even think I heard one of them whistle. I scanned the audience for Elliot; he was sitting in the back, a stony expression on his face.

I looked down at my speech. Thankfully, it was short. All I had to do was run up there, recite it, and leave. It would be embarrassing to lose, but there was no shame, I told myself, in getting crushed by someone like Ashley. She had worked so hard for so many months and she clearly wanted this more than I did. And she had probably put in a ton of hours to get that scoreboard, even though Mr. Hendricks had probably done most of the paperwork.

I was already rehearsing how I would break the news to my parents when the electrician faced me—and nodded. He walked out the door before I could get a better look at his face. But even with the bald cap and mustache, I could tell: It was James.

"Ladies and gentlemen," Ashley announced. "Without further ado, I present the new scoreboard for your *Glendale Lions!*"

She yanked off the sheet and the applause gradually died down. I couldn't see the scoreboard from where I was sitting, but I could see Ashley's face: Her skin had turned pale and her eyes were round with horror. One or two boys began chuckling and the laughter spread like dominoes across the rows of the auditorium. Ashley looked around frantically for the electrician, but of course he had already left.

I craned my neck and took a peek at the scoreboard. It was completely blank, except for a gigantic tiger and the words GO WEST SIDE PREP.

Ashley mumbled something about it being a mix-up and slinked back to her seat. Then the principal banged his gavel, to stop the uproar, and announced my name. I read through the speech one more time, put it in my pocket and walked up to the podium.

"I haven't done as much research as my opponent," I recited, "and I don't have as much knowledge about school policy. But there's one thing I do know: The Lions rule!"

I put on the hat and awkwardly started chanting.

"Lions! Lions! Lions!"

"Lions!" Elliot shouted, muffling his voice with a handkerchief. "Lions!"

A couple other boys joined in, including Lance, and before

long, everyone was chanting. Everyone except for Ashley, of course. I kept on chanting as I watched her slip silently through the door and race toward the solitude of the bathroom.

• • •

"Congrats," Lance said. "That speech was awesome."

He stuck out a fist and I awkwardly bumped it with my own.

"I have a pretty sweet idea for basketball uniforms," he said. "I'll save you a seat tomorrow at lunch."

Elliot and I walked down the stairs, toward the lobby. I felt guilty about what had happened to Ashley, but there wasn't time to give it much thought. Too many people were congratulating me on my victory.

"How did you know that would work?" I asked Elliot.

"Because people are animals," he said. "All you have to do is treat them like—"

"Hey Seymour!"

I turned around and Jessica was in front of me, in yellow shorts and a low-cut tank top. A teacher had handed her a sweatshirt and track pants during the assembly, but evidently, she had never gotten around to changing into them. She laid the gym clothes on a nearby chair and threw her bare arms around me.

"Congratulations!" she said. "I have some ideas for dances— let's talk soon!"

She scooped up her gym clothes and made her way to the bathroom, turning around once to smile at me.

"Oh my God," I said.

"Listen to me," Elliot said. "Now that you're sitting at Lance's table, I'll need to teach you some basic power moves."

"Did you see that?" I whispered.

"Make sure to sit on Lance's *left*. If you sit on his right, he'll never consider you a real threat. That goes back to the days of hand-to-hand combat. If you're holding a sword in your right hand, you want your rivals on your left, to make it easier to slash them with your sword."

"I can't believe she wants to talk to me about dances! Do you think that means she'll call me on the phone?"

"If Lance starts telling a story, stand up and go to the bathroom without saying anything. I know that doesn't *sound* particularly aggressive, but trust me, it'll send a message. And never turn your tray sidewise! The table is a piece of territory and you need to claim as much of it as possible."

That's when it occurred to me: I would be leaving Elliot all alone at the third table.

"Hey," I said. "Why don't you sit with us tomorrow?"

Elliot stopped in his tracks.

"What?"

"Come on," I said. "I bet they'll let you squeeze in. I mean, if I tell them you're my friend and all, I'm sure I could get you a spot."

Elliot's eyes narrowed.

"*You* . . . could get *me* . . . a spot?"

"Sure?" I said. "Why not?"

Elliot clenched his jaw and breathed tensely through his nose. I started to apologize, but before I could get any words out, he spun around and headed for the street. He was moving so fast that I doubt he noticed Ashley, who was standing by his limo, staring at the face in the driver's seat window.

• • •

"I think it's just wonderful," my mom said. "Mr. Ninth-Grade President!"

"You're going to have a blast," my father said. "Just remember—power corrupts!"

He and my mother started to laugh, but were quickly interrupted by the ringing of the phone. My mother headed to the kitchen to answer it.

"It might be Jessica," I said.

My father stared at me, in shock.

"Who's Jessica?"

"Just a girl I know."

My father coughed—he had been drinking a glass of water.

"You want to know something?" he said, after he had recovered. "I'm super proud of you. When I was your age, I never would have had the maturity to put myself out there like that. And now you're meeting new people, making new friends."

"Lance said I could sit with him at lunch tomorrow," I said.

"That's great," my dad said. "Is he a cool guy?"

I shrugged.

"He's probably the most powerful person in the grade."

He squinted at me. We didn't say anything else until my mother returned and started to clear the dishes.

"Who was that?" I asked.

"Nothing," she said, forcing an odd laugh. "It was just . . . something crazy."

She rolled her eyes.

"Ashley's *mother*," she said.

"What did she have to say?" my father asked.

"Oh, it's just ridiculous. She thinks you and Elliot arranged some kind of . . . I can't even say it, it's so silly."

"Arranged some kind of what?"

"*I* don't know," she said. "A *conspiracy* or something. Some people are just sore losers."

She smiled softly at me.

"Seymour, you don't have any idea what that woman's talking about . . . do you?"

My dad looked across the table at me.

"Do you?" he asked.

"No!" I said. "Of course not."

I grabbed another slice of brisket from the platter in an effort to act casual, but they kept staring at me while I sliced up the meat, with an expression I had never seen before. I didn't realize until I was about to swallow that I had taken the last piece.

PART TWO

Go to Jail

HARVARD APPLICATION

Name: Seymour Herson
Place of Birth: New York City
Current Standing: Glendale Preparatory School, 12th Grade
GPA: 4.0
Ethnicity: Caucasian, Native American (see supplement, "Official Genezaro Indian Tribal Document")
Primary Household Earner's Occupation: Associate Professor of Economics, Bishop House Author

Please list your principal extracurricular activities and hobbies in the order of their interest to you. Include specific events and/or major accomplishments.

Activities	Year/s Involved	Hrs/wk	Describe Details
Anti-Asbestos Activist	9,10,11,12	20	Served Community
Class President	9,10,11,12	20	Developed Leadership Skills
Independent lab research	9,10,11,12	4	Attempting to cure Pasternak-Schwarzschild's disease
Painter	9,10,11,12	20	Composed abstract works (see supplement "Green Waters")

Have you ever been found responsible for a disciplinary violation?
No.
Have you ever been convicted of any crime?
No.

Please write an essay on a topic of your choice. This personal essay helps us to become acquainted with you as a person, apart from courses, grades, and test scores.

"Necklace of Hope"

by Seymour Herson

When people tell me that it's impossible to make a difference, and that I should give up hope for this world, I just close my eyes and think about the greatest teacher I ever had. He didn't teach me how to take integrations or write bibliographies. In fact, he couldn't even read or write. But I learned enough from him to fill a thousand textbooks. His classroom was the street. And his subject? It was life.

To most people, Hal Sagal was just a typical homeless person. A "bum" or "vagrant" to be ignored, spat on, and forgotten. But from the moment I first met him, under a bridge, I knew that a great wisdom lay behind his leathery, rubicund face.

My classmates told me I was crazy.

"Why do you spend so much time with that man?" they said. "He's just a homeless person."

Just a homeless person. What did they know about the wars Hal had fought in? Or the animals he cared for, nursing them back to health under his bridge?

It's easy to grow cynical in this world. And there was a time when I would have listened to my classmates and turned my back on Hal. But that was before he got sick and taught me his most important lesson yet.

I spent three months by his side during that cruel winter, bringing him food, blankets, and, perhaps most importantly, a hand to hold.

"Please let me take you to the hospital!" I begged. "Or at least tell the authorities about you!"

But he just shook his wise head and smiled. At first I didn't understand. But now I realize: When you've lived a life as full as Hal's, you have nothing to fear.

Just before Hal passed, he took off his wooden necklace and pressed it into my hands. It may not be the most fashionable accessory. But I'll wear it proudly for the rest of my life.

That's *my* diploma.

Academic Recommendation

In all my years of teaching French, I have never seen a student undergo a transformation as dramatic as Seymour's. When he first entered my classroom, as a seventh-grader, he lagged so far behind the other students that I wrote a letter to his parents encouraging them to have him tested for learning disabilities. He consistently flunked his exams, including rudimentary vocabulary quizzes on common nouns.

At some point in the eighth grade, though, Seymour "turned things around." With an abruptness I still can't fully understand, he transformed himself from a flunking student into an A-plus superstar.

Seymour has a natural grasp of French that one rarely finds outside of France. It's not just his test scores—which are immaculate. It's his conversational instincts. In oral exams, he seems to know instinctively what I plan to ask him in advance. On several occasions this year, he cut me off with the correct answer before I even finished reading him my question! If that's not fluency, I don't know what is.

Seymour is such a talented linguist that I worry sometimes that my class is stunting his progress. He has confessed to me in private that he feels uncomfortable speaking spontaneously in class, because he doesn't want to embarrass his fellow students with a show of his superior fluency. I hope that at Harvard he will find an environment better suited to his gifts.

Sincerely,
Mr. Hendricks

Outside Recommendation

I like this one.
—T. Allagash

I certify that all information submitted in the admission process—including the application and the personal essay—is my own work, factually true, and honestly presented.

Signature:
Seymour Herson

DECISION: ACCEPTED.

• • •

"Hey Elliot? What does rubicund mean?"

"It doesn't mean anything. It's a nonsense word."

"Come on. It's got to mean *something.*"

Elliot polished his cue and knocked in a bank shot.

"You want to know what rubicund means?" Elliot said. "It means, 'I know what rubicund means.' *That's* what it means!"

"I can't believe they fell for that essay. It couldn't have been more ridiculous."

"What do you expect?" Elliot said. "The college application has become nothing more than an exercise in self-degradation! A groveling apology from a liberal middle class that feels guilty for a power they only *think* they possess! Anyway . . . congratulations."

I walked over to the dumbwaiter.

"Want a drink?"

"I already have several," he said.

I nodded and sent down for a Scotch, in a tall glass with lemon.

"Hey, Elliot, can you get me a single next year? Those dorm rooms in the yard look tiny."

"I'm pretty sure they're assigned randomly."

"Randomly?" I laughed. "Come on Elliot, there's got to be an angle. What about disability? We could always say I have Crohn's."

"I think they'd notice when you arrived at school without the disease."

"If I got caught, we could blame it on a faulty diagnosis! Pay some doctor to say he mixed up the tubes!"

Elliot smiled proudly.

"What's the game count?" he asked.

"I think we're tied," I said.

"How about that?"

The dumbwaiter creaked back up with my drink, as well as a large basket of pastries.

"That damn chef," Elliot muttered. "He's the biggest boot-licker my father ever hired."

I grabbed a croissant and bit into its warm, flaky shell. A jet of malted fudge oozed into my mouth. It was so rich that I had to sit down. I'd known Elliot for four years, but I was still occasionally shocked by the luxuries that surrounded him.

"New chef?" I asked.

Elliot sighed.

"It's a long and ridiculous story."

I took another bite of the croissant and waited for Elliot to tell it to me.

"Last year, after Terry's second heart attack, his doctors pleaded with him to appoint a full-time personal trainer. He eventually hired some German to get them off his back—a former Olympian named Dolf. But on the same day, he hired Passard."

"Who?"

"Jacques Passard. He is arguably the greatest pastry chef of his generation."

"Jesus," I said, my mouth full of crumbs. "Do these guys know about each other?"

"Are you kidding?" Elliot said. "Terry's favorite hobby is pitting them against each other. They *live* in the same apartment. No more interruptions."

I finished off the croissant and grabbed another.

"Terry pays them a modest base salary," Elliot explained. "But the bulk of their income comes from performance-based bonuses."

"What do you mean?"

"Every month, Terry goes to their apartment and writes out an enormous check. Then he steps onto a scale. If he's lost weight since his last visit, he gives the check to the trainer. If he's gained weight, he gives it to the chef."

"So they're constantly at war."

Elliot nodded.

"You should see the look on Dolf's face when Jacques makes meringue. His cheeks turn bright red and the muscles stand out in his neck. Those two men hate each other more than you could possibly imagine."

As Elliot racked up the next game, it occurred to me that he had never mentioned either of his father's heart attacks. I wanted to ask him how serious they were, but of course I knew better.

I offered Elliot a pastry and he waved me off with his usual flick of the wrist. I wondered if Elliot had his own team of doctors. If he did, he certainly wasn't listening to any of their advice. Every time I visited him, he seemed smaller and weaker than ever. For a while, I assumed it was an optical illusion. I was going through a drastic growth spurt, and everyone in the class seemed to be shrinking. But no one was shrinking as dramatically as Elliot. He usually wore a new outfit every day, but occasionally I recognized a pair of pants from two or even three years ago. And once, I could have sworn that I saw him sporting the same pair of boat shoes he had worn on his very first day at Glendale, back in the eighth grade. It was possible, I thought sometimes, that he hadn't changed at all.

Elliot turned around to break, and I took the opportunity to jot down the word "rubicund," so I wouldn't forget it. At some point, toward the end of eighth grade, I had started to carry around a thick red notebook in my pocket. Elliot always knew about Mr. Hendricks's pop quizzes in advance, and I wanted to have the dates on hand so that I would know when to study. Before long, I was writing down the questions, too—and from there, it didn't take me long to move on to the answers. I didn't feel guilty. French was obviously a useless language. If anything, cheating at it was *improving* my capacity to learn by allowing me to focus on my other, more worthwhile classes.

By tenth grade I was cheating in every class, including, somehow, pottery. And by senior year, I was filling the notebook with information that had nothing to do with school. There were summaries of books I was supposed to have read, meanings of paintings I was supposed to have created, spellings of diseases I was supposed to be trying to cure, and a shockingly long list of homeless people whom I had supposedly befriended. The notebook became so incriminating that I developed a habit of frisking my pocket every couple of minutes to make sure it was still on my person. I wanted to destroy it, but I couldn't: There was too much to keep track of.

I occasionally felt guilty about my success, but on the whole it felt deserved. It wasn't like I hadn't worked hard. Perpetuating so many lies was difficult, and I was doing it all on my own. Or *mostly* on my own.

I got a call on my cell, and even though Elliot was hunched over the pool table and my phone was set on vibrate, he noticed.

"Don't answer," he said.

I waited until the ringing stopped and flicked it open so I could hear my new voice mail.

"Speaker," Elliot demanded.

I laid the phone on the table and we listened together, in silence.

"Hey, man. I know I already left you a message, but I want to make sure you knew that the party's still going. I know you're probably busy, but everyone keeps asking where you're at, so I guess they want to see you. Anyway, if you need the address, give me a call."

I picked up the phone and was about to dial when Elliot snapped his fingers.

"What do you think you're doing?"

"Calling back Lance," I said. "That's the third time he's called."

"All the more reason to ignore his calls! I mean, honestly, do you realize how pathetic that is?"

"Well, yeah, but . . . it's his birthday."

"If he hadn't called you or invited you, than *maybe* his party would be worth attending."

"So I should only go to parties that people don't invite me to?"

"You shouldn't go to *any* parties," Elliot said, "if you can help it."

"I already promised him I'd go," I said. "What am I going to tell him?"

"Nothing," Elliot said. "The more evasive you are about your activities, the more impressive people will assume them to be. We've been over this a thousand times."

"But if I never go to parties, won't people stop inviting me? I mean, it's the middle of senior year and I still haven't really been to any."

"Of course you haven't been to any," he said. "You're far too popular."

I laughed.

"I never hang out with anybody, Elliot, ever. I'm only popular on paper."

"What other kind of popular is there?"

He dashed off a note and tossed it into the dumbwaiter.

"I'm going to show you something," he said. "It's the most desired and envied artifact in the entire Allagash collection."

"Can you show it to me after the party?"

He ignored me and spun the wheel. The box landed downstairs with a thud, and a few seconds later I heard the sound of running, followed by an elaborate series of clicks and snaps.

"We keep it locked up," Elliot explained.

There were some more clicks and snaps. Then the wheel creaked in the opposite direction and the box returned.

Elliot took a long and lazy sip from his martini. I could tell he was deliberately stalling.

"Come on," I said, finally. "What's in there?"

He took another slow sip, and then, finally, he opened the box.

It contained a small, heavily rusted key. It was dark green with brown splotches, but I could tell that it used to be gold or silver.

"Have you ever heard of the Seven Circles Club?" he asked me.

"Of course not," I said.

"Then listen closely," he said. "And no interruptions."

• • •

Before it was completely destroyed in the Great Fire of 1835, the Seven Circles Club dominated New York's cultural scene. There were plenty of prominent gentlemen's clubs in those days. The Excelsior Club was so wealthy that two of its bathroom attendants became noted philanthropists after their retirement. And the Vanitas Club was so old that its address—24 Rum Way—no longer referred to an existing street. But the Seven Circles was older and richer than all of them— and far more exclusive. A club's status is usually measured by the number of luminaries it attracts. But the Seven Circles Club was less famous for the people it let in than for the people it rejected. In its first ten years of business, the governing board denied membership to three millionaires, five U.S. senators, the man who cured scurvy, Lewis and Clark, and George Washington's only son.

"Why'd they reject *him*?" I asked.

"Because his father was a farmer," Elliot said.

The Seven Circles occupied a dome-shaped building on the site of Peter Stuyvesant's original mansion. It was comprised of seven concentric circles, nested within one another, like the rings of Saturn. The outermost layer was as decadent as any club in New York, Paris, or London. The circular walls were plastered with masterworks from the Renaissance. Liveried butlers walked in a continuous loop, offering members imported British gin and cigarettes from Turkey. But the first circle was practically monastic compared to the second circle. Of the club's forty members, only twenty had keys to the giant brass door that led into the next ring-shaped room.

Once inside the next compartment, members were treated to French absinthe, Brazilian cocaine, and a display of *real* Renaissance paintings. (The first circle's paintings, it turned out, were clever forgeries—a prank on the less prestigious members of the club.)

Only ten members had keys to the third circle. It was adorned with stained glass and Christian relics, and unlike the first two circles, it lacked servants of any kind. It was within *this* circle that members learned the true mission of the Seven Circles Club: to reject evil and embrace Christ. The room was lined with granite kneelers so members could supplicate and pray for the sins they had committed before ascending to the third circle.

The fourth circle was an opium den. The five men with keys smoked out of ruby pipes, slept with whores from the Orient, and congratulated one another on the hilarious prank they had pulled on the fools still stranded in the third circle.

The fifth circle was made out of wood from Judean palm trees, which have been extinct since the time of Caesar. The sixth, somewhat predictably, was made out of *real* Judean palm trees. And the seventh room—well, that was open to debate. One contemporary minister held that it contained a piece of the True Cross. And a pair of Columbia University scientists insisted that it contained the last dodo, still alive but struggling on a largely gin-based diet. There were plenty of rumors, but the only man who knew its contents with certainty, the only member of the Seven Circles who possessed the coveted seventh key, was the founder himself, Elliot's ancestor—the first American Allagash!

"So what was in the seventh room?"

"A *stool*," Elliot announced triumphantly, "made out of wood."

"Extinct wood?"

"What? No. Regular wood."

"Oh."

Elliot blinked a few times, exasperated by my reaction.

"Don't you get it?" he said. "The contents were irrelevant! The only thing that mattered was the thickness of the walls, the impregnability of the lock! Four different men tried to assassinate Cornelius just to obtain the key. It's rumored that he started the Great Fire *himself,* to make sure his club would burn before anyone knew the truth. He spent up to eight hours a day in that little room, gaining power and prestige with every passing second— just by sitting there! *That* is how the game is played!"

I imagined Elliot's ancestor sitting alone in the dark, surrounded by the sounds of laughter and clinking glasses.

"Wouldn't it be more fun to hang out in a different room? Like the one with opium?"

Elliot tossed the key back into the dumbwaiter and sat down, exhausted.

Lance called again and my phone skittered awkwardly across the wooden table.

"Go ahead," Elliot wheezed. "What do I care?"

• • •

"Keep going," I told the cab driver.

"This is Seventy-sixth and Lex," he said.

"Um . . . I meant Seventy-fifth."

I got out of the cab, stood behind a tree, and watched my class-mates stroll in and out of Lance's brownstone. It was two forty-five in the morning, but music still blared from the second-floor window. Lance had invited the entire grade and almost everyone had shown up.

I got invited to lots of parties, but Elliot always convinced me not to go to them. I argued with him occasionally, but he never ran out of points to make. He'd rant for hours about the "low sta-tion" of the other guests, referring to them alternately as "animals" and "garbage animals." Usually, by the time he was finished with his tirade, it was too late to go anywhere and I would just spend the night at Elliot's.

But Elliot couldn't keep me away from Lance's birthday party. It was the biggest event of the year. He had distributed fliers. If I didn't go to this party, which one would I go to? In school, my so-cial interactions consisted primarily of people approaching me in the hall and congratulating me on things (like getting reelected as class president, getting into Harvard, or saving a homeless man's life). Elliot had urged me to remain as aloof from the student body as possible—and I understood his logic. But sometimes, while rushing through the halls, I'd hear two people laughing about something that had happened at a party, and I'd feel left out, even if it was a party I'd been invited to.

I checked my hair in the window of a parked car and stepped out from behind the tree. Some of my classmates were sitting on the stoop, exchanging cell-phone numbers with kids from different schools. I even recognized kids from other grades— juniors, sophomores, even a couple of freshmen. How cool could a party be if there were freshmen?

I checked my hair again. I had recently started going to Elliot's hairstylist, an intense salon owner from Milan. I could tell he had given me a good haircut because it had taken him four hours, and when he was finished, his assistants had taken photographs. But the haircut was really difficult to maintain. I was supposed to rub some kind of gel into the sides every morning, and I had to go downtown every Saturday for a touch-up.

It was almost three in the morning. If I showed up to the party this late, the kids on the stoop would definitely ask me where I had been. I would need a pretty exciting answer to justify such extreme lateness. Maybe I could tell them I had been at some other, more impressive party? Or that I had become engrossed in some important book? But what if they asked me follow-up questions? I didn't know about any other parties going on that night and I hadn't read a book in months. I retreated behind the tree to think things over.

The truth was, Lance's party had pretty much ended. It would be pointless to show up just as everyone else was leaving. One thing was clear: I couldn't stay where I was for much longer. If someone spotted me hiding, the night would be a total catastrophe. My stomach lurched: What if they had already spotted me? What if they were watching me right now?

I took out my cell phone and pretended to make a call—so that if people *were* watching, they would assume I was attending to some kind of important business.

Never mind, I imagined one of the guests saying. *I was wrong— he's not hiding behind that tree. He's just making a phone call, on his way to the party.*

Oh, you're right. That Seymour guy's really busy, huh?

Yeah. That's why he always comes to parties so late, or not at all.

I scrunched up my eyebrows and nodded solemnly.

Look at that. He just heard some kind of urgent news.

I wonder who he's talking to? Probably someone important, if it's this late at night. Like a celebrity.

Hey look at that . . . he's turning around and leaving.

He's moving fast.

I guess he has somewhere important to be and it can't wait another second.

That's too bad. I was really looking forward to hanging out with him.

We all were.

My breathing slowed to its normal pace as the music faded behind me. I scurried around the corner and stuffed my cell phone into my pocket. What the hell had happened back there?

"Seymour?"

Lance stomped out a cigarette while Jessica threw her arms around me.

"I can't believe we missed you! We just went out for a smoke."

"Must have lost track of time," Lance said, smirking.

Lance had gotten into some decent schools, I'd heard, but had rejected them all in order to play basketball for a Division II team. He was still the tallest kid in the class. And even though I was gaining on him, I could still see his nostrils.

"So," he said, "how's my party going?"

"Great!" I said. "Just really . . . great."

Jessica curled her arms around Lance's waist.

"Did you see Lance play?"

"My band did a few songs," he said. "Mostly covers."

"It was awesome," Jessica said. "And they gave out *shirts.*"

She twirled around a couple of times to model the one she had on. It was bright pink and looked as if it had been designed for a toddler. She was wearing a new jewel on her belly-button ring.

Teachers no longer punished Jessica for dress-code violations. Monitoring her offenses had become too exhausting and at a certain point, they had simply given up. Jessica still managed to land herself in detention from time to time, however, with Lance's help. The couple had received their first PDA (public display of affection) citation sometime in the ninth grade. By senior year, they had accumulated so many that whenever a teacher shouted "Hey!" in the hallway, students instinctively glanced in their direction to see what kind of physical offense they were committing.

"We changed the name of our band," Lance said. "We're called the Fuzz now."

"That's a cool name," I said.

"I *told* you," Jessica whispered to him.

Lance rolled his eyes, clearly annoyed that Jessica had cast me as an authority on band names.

"I don't know," he said. "We might change it again."

I tried not to stare as Lance slid his hand down the back of Jessica's jeans. He had begun with just his fingertips, but now most of his palm was inserted. My throat felt dry and constricted as I watched him inch farther and farther down. Eventually, I realized that Jessica was saying something to me.

"How's research going?"

"What?"

"You know," she said. "Research, for that disease? The one you're trying to cure?"

"Oh!" I said. "It's, you know . . . it's complicated."

Jessica nodded solemnly. I could tell that she respected me, or at least the things I claimed to have achieved. But I was still just as nervous around her as I had been in the eighth grade. I was juggling so many lies and every time she spoke to me, I feared the entire act would come crashing down.

"It's probably way over our heads," she said.

I didn't know how to respond, so I just stared back at her in silence.

"Well, we're all rooting for you," Lance said, tugging Jessica's arm. "Listen, we should probably head back—"

"Yeah," I said. "No—me too. I've got a lot of stuff to do."

I shook their hands awkwardly and watched them turn the corner, hand in hand. The moment they were out of sight, my phone started to ring. I didn't bother to check the screen: Who else could it be?

"How was Lance's party?" he asked. "Carefree and fun?"

I thought, for a moment, about lying to him. But he had already started to laugh—a loud, insane cackle—and I could tell that, somehow, he already knew exactly what had happened.

• • •

My father's wheelbarrow lay on its side, frozen in its pathetic final pose. A five and a six had sent him rocketing across the board, from his peaceful Water Works plant to the lobby of the Hotel Boardwalk. His bills lay in a messy, multicolored pile. There'd been no need to count them: He was ruined.

I could picture my father cradling the dice in his palm, begging God for a pair of sixes—the breathless silence as he flung them across the board—and then my mother leaping to her feet, laughing and clapping and demanding her two thousand dollars. She'd gloat for a second or two—and then completely switch gears, kissing my father on the cheek, cursing his awful luck.

I had outgrown Monopoly Night sometime in middle school, but my parents still played every Friday. They always left the board out until Saturday morning, just in case I wanted to see how their game had ended. I usually barreled right past it on my way home, annoyed that they thought I would care about something so childish. But in recent weeks I had caught myself studying the board, sometimes for a long time, trying to piece together what I'd missed.

I walked through the living room and made my way down the hallway. It was a new apartment, with more rooms than the last one, and I was still getting used to all the light switches. I slapped at the walls for a while, then gave up and thrust out my arms like

a blind man. Within seconds, I had fallen over some boxes of photos that my mom was in the process of hanging. I cursed, punched
the wall, and crawled into my bedroom.

By the time I found the light switch, my parents were standing
in the doorway.

"Everything okay?"

"Yes," I said. "Good night."

"Sorry for barging in," my dad said. "We just heard you . . . in
the hall. It sounded bad."

"Yeah, well, I'm okay."

"Are you hungry?" my mom asked. "There's brisket."

"I ate at Elliot's."

My parents nodded.

"You missed a pretty fun game," my dad said. "Did you check
out the board?"

"No."

"Oh. Well . . . it was a good one. Mom won."

It dawned on me that this was the longest conversation we had
had in months. It's not that they weren't interested in my life:
They hung on my every word, like mediums at a séance. But they
rarely asked me any questions. They had so many, I imagined,
that they didn't know where to begin.

When I announced one day that I would be going with Elliot
to Harvard, they were silent for almost a minute. I had applied
early, without telling them, and it was the first time they'd heard
me mention it. They congratulated me profusely, of course, but I
could detect a hint of fear in their voice. It was as if I had announced I was actually an alien and had received orders to return

to my home planet. They signed the forms I gave them and ordered me a pair of crimson sweatshirts. But they never asked to see my application.

I started to close my door, but my father blocked it with his forearm.

"You dropped something," my mother said, squeezing her hand through the gap.

I snatched the red notebook from her hand and quickly shut the door. My heart pumped wildly, as a terrifying thought occurred to me: *They could have read it if they had wanted to.* And then I had an even scarier thought.

They hadn't.

• • •

"Harvard is a fine place, Seymour. And I believe you'll fit in there, better than I did at first. I know this sounds strange, but when I entered Harvard, I actually had some genuine academic interests! It's true: I enrolled in very traditional courses—a philosophy seminar, a history elective, even a class about economics. But I had a pretty rigid drinking schedule to stick to, and I soon found out that my classes interfered with it.

"Luckily, my club mates introduced me to a different kind of Harvard course—the kind designed to accommodate the needs of the wealthy. There were several of these courses, and with the exception of a few illiterate football players, their enrollments were made up entirely of fuel and shipping heirs. One of the classes was called Boats. Its actual title was a little longer—Atlantic Exploration, or something in that vein—I never actually found out.

The course was taught by an eighty-five-year-old professor named Sherwood, whose father had donated over a dozen libraries to Harvard in the late nineteenth century. He lectured twice a week, from four until about four fifteen. He discussed different explorers and their boats, but often spiraled off into other topics, such as the history of his mansion and the 'immigrant problem.' He drank openly during class and occasionally smoked as well. His lectures were difficult to follow, but we enjoyed his spirited delivery, and whenever he threw his hands up in the air to signal the end of a lecture, we applauded.

"Attendance was required, but the course's only actual assignment was a ten-page paper, due at the end of the semester, about 'any topic related to the class lectures.' For most courses, graduating members of my club passed down their term papers to younger members, to retype and hand in as their own. But there were so many of us enrolled in Boats each year that we felt the need to restrain ourselves. We couldn't *all* hand in old papers—even an eighty-five-year-old would catch on. So we limited ourselves to one plagiarized paper each term. It was called 'The Fishing Habits of Henry Hudson.' The club secretary kept the original in a glass case, and every year, on the night before the due date, we had a drinking contest to determine who got to hand it in. It was a generic essay, with a bland thesis and a forgettable conclusion. The only distinctive thing about it was the cover, which featured a crude school-boy drawing of a fish. It was an incredibly unnecessary flourish, but we always dutifully redrew it and handed it in along with the ten retyped pages. By the time I enrolled in Boats, the paper had been turned in by thirty club members, and each of them had received an A-minus.

"I won the drinking contest handily and spent the early morning in the club library, drinking Irish coffee so I could stay awake long enough to retype the paper. I stopped short of redrawing the fish, but I managed to transcribe all the words and the footnotes, and with ten minutes till the deadline, I strolled to the yard and dropped it off.

"Our papers arrived at the club two months later, by mail. Professor Sherwood had written lengthy, indecipherable rants in the margins of everybody's essays that seemed unrelated to the essays themselves, and he had given everyone a passing grade. I was about to follow everyone back into the poker room when I found *my* exam, or at least the one that I had turned in. I checked the grade, tossed it aside—and then picked it back up again. I couldn't believe it. The old man had given me a B-plus.

"I flipped through the paper, looking for comments, but the margins were blank. The only words he had written were on the last page. It was a single sentence, scrawled hurriedly with a fountain pen:

" 'Where's the fish?'

"So you see, Seymour, you're sure to fit in. It's really the only place for you!"

• • •

"Why did you tell everyone I was trying to cure that crazy disease?"

"I didn't tell *everyone*. I told a local newspaper."

"You told *The New York Times*."

"That's local. Waiter?"

A man in a waistcoat marched over, pad in hand.

"I'll have a Bloody Mary."

The waiter hesitated.

"I'm sorry, Mr. Allagash," he said. "But the bartender doesn't get here until nine."

Elliot rolled his eyes.

"Wake him."

I took my French vocabulary book out of my backpack and Elliot immediately grabbed it.

"What's all this?"

"There's going to be a pop quiz first period," I said. "And I need to ace it. Mr. Hendricks is getting suspicious."

"I find that hard to believe. The man wrote you a positively glowing recommendation."

"Elliot, this is serious. I got stuck in an elevator with him yesterday, and he started talking to me in French, and I had no idea what he was saying. I'm *sure* he could tell I was lost."

Elliot laughed.

"My God, you're helpless," he said. "I go to Paris for four days and the dominoes begin to fall."

"You were in Paris? What were you doing in *Paris*?"

He shrugged.

"What am I doing in *New York*?"

The waiter brought him his Bloody Mary and he ordered a second one before even tasting the first.

"You go to *school* here," I reminded him. "You're a full-time student at a high school."

Elliot waved his hand dismissively.

"Don't remind me."

For the past four years, Elliot had gone to great lengths to spare himself the indignity of attending high school. In the ninth and tenth grades, he feigned a series of increasingly rare diseases, beginning with cadmium poisoning and culminating in Saint Vitus's dance. But it required a lot of time and research to come up with new illnesses and get hold of the proper medical forgeries, and eventually, he got tired of it. By senior year he had settled on a diagnosis of plain old mono, supplemented by the occasional "overseas funeral." Elliot attended school only thirty-six days a year—the bare minimum for graduating—and he went through them in a state of such incredible intoxication that by the following day he often had a valid reason to stay home.

"These *appearances* are killing me," he said. "Who am I? The queen in peacetime England?"

"We should probably go soon," I said, taking back my French book. "We're going to be late."

Elliot flagged down the waiter and I sighed with relief. It was already quarter of eight, but if we left within five minutes, and traffic was light, James could probably get us to school before the first bell. I had almost finished zipping my backpack when I realized Elliot was ordering his third Bloody Mary.

"In a tall glass this time," he told the waiter. "And hold the garnishes."

He laughed.

"Who are we kidding?" he said. "Hold the tomato juice, too."

I slammed down my fist and our dishes rattled softly against the tablecloth. The waiter looked up from his pad, and Elliot slowly turned toward me.

"Please," I mumbled. "We're going to be late."

Elliot whipped out his pocket watch and grinned.

"Well, I'll be," he said. "Seymour, why didn't you say something?"

"Does James know we had breakfast at the St. Regis?" I said. "You've got to call him."

Elliot nodded and reached into his waistcoat, only to pull out a flask. I cursed under my breath and took out my own cell phone.

"What's his number?" I demanded.

Elliot shrugged.

"He usually just *arrives*," he said. "My personal deus ex machina!"

He stared quizzically at his flask.

"Would you like to hear something interesting?" he said. "I stole this flask. I was in a shop in London and I stole it. There were many bystanders, but I had James distract them with a diversion. Isn't that an incredible story?"

He took a long swig.

"The Scotch inside it is also stolen," he said. "That was some afternoon."

"Goddamn it," I said. "We're taking the subway."

Elliot giggled.

"The what?"

I grabbed his knobby wrist and led him toward the entrance of

the Fifty-ninth Street station. By the time we made it to the escalator, his wiry limbs were writhing with laughter.

"You mean the *underground*?"

I don't know why it surprised me that Elliot had never been on
the subway before. It would have been more surprising if he had.

I pulled some crumpled singles out of my pocket and hastily
smoothed them against the side of the MetroCard dispenser. I
tried to feed them into the slot, but the machine kept spitting
them back out at me.

"Elliot, do you have any singles?"

"Any what?"

"Nevermind," I said.

I found some quarters in my backpack and bought us a couple
of one-way passes. When I looked back at Elliot, he was standing
on top of a nearby bench, surveying the terminal with wonder,
like an explorer in a newly discovered tomb. He squinted at a
framed map.

"So it connects with the buses?" he said. "How clever!"

He pointed at a group of men in work clothes, marching off to
repair some segment of the track.

"Look at them go!" he exclaimed. "Like a colony of mice!"

One of the workers started to turn around, and I quickly pulled
Elliot off the bench.

"I hear a train coming," I said. "Come on."

I handed Elliot his pass. He held it up to the light and examined it, as one would a piece of foreign currency. The train roared
into the station.

"Come on!" I shouted.

154 • ELLIOT ALLAGASH

I rushed through the turnstile and sprinted toward the closest car. As the doors closed, I stuck my wrists inside, and a couple of strangers grabbed hold of them. After a tense moment, the doors parted again and I was yanked into the car. The other passengers burst into applause as the train went into motion. An elderly woman patted me on the shoulder.

"That was a close one!" she said, laughing.

Just before the train left the station, I caught sight of Elliot, standing at the foot of the escalator. It was going the wrong way; he would have to take the stairs. He shook his head a couple times in disbelief. Then he grabbed the railing, and started off alone.

• • •

I ran down the hall and burst into French class, my pen already drawn.

"Did I miss it?"

Mr. Hendricks stared at me.

"What do you mean, Seymour?" he asked, scrunching up his forehead. "Miss what?"

What the hell was I doing? It was a pop quiz. I wasn't even supposed to know about its existence.

I cleared my throat.

"Did I miss the *lesson,*" I said, emphatically.

His eyes lit up.

"Oh!" he said. "Oh! No, Seymour. You're just in time!"

I could hear my classmates groaning as I took my customary seat in the center of the front row. It was moments like these that made me question Elliot's definition of the word *popular.* I'd gone from the bottom rung of his status list to the very top. But the two slots seemed to have a lot in common.

Mr. Hendricks locked eyes with me and launched into one of his rapid-fire gibberish monologues. I smiled and nodded until he handed me my quiz. Then I filled it out, handed it in, and got out of there as fast as I could.

I compared the incident to all the other close calls of the month; it didn't even rank among the top five. There had been a bunch of horrible moments in math class when the teacher went out for a smoke and asked me to lead the lesson in his absence. And then there'd been that nightmare conversation in the cafeteria with the lunch lady.

"I just want to thank you for everything you're doing, Seymour. You know, my uncle suffers from Pasternak-Schwarzschild's disease."

"Oh! I'm sorry to hear that. Is he in good spirits?"

"He's in a coma. I mean . . . obviously. It's Pasternak-Schwarzschild's disease."

"Right. Of course. Right."

I ducked into the back stairwell and slowly made my way up to the roof.

• • •

Students weren't allowed on the roof, and the administration seemed serious about enforcing the rule. They'd lined the upper stairwell with security cameras, and if someone spotted you on the monitor, you faced an automatic suspension. But with the help of one of Elliot's maps, I'd figured out an alternate route. First I took the back stairwell down to the boiler room. Then I walked through the janitor's storage room, past the rows of retired mops. There, hidden behind a discarded bookshelf, lay the entrance to the school's old steam tunnels. At that point, all I had to do was enter the combination—I don't know how Elliot had gotten it— and go up a whole bunch of ladders. After about ten minutes of climbing, the tunnel would spit me out of a steam vent, which hadn't been operational in eighty years, since the school had stopped relying on coal heat.

The roof itself was bare, except for a water tower and some pipes. You could see both rivers and most of the park and the traffic was so remote, not even the most ghastly car crash could startle you very much. The black tar surface was always warm from the sunlight—but never hot. It took me about twenty-five minutes to get up there, and I went once a day, at least.

When I first discovered the route, I was so proud of myself that I immediately called up Elliot to brag about my findings. But when he picked up the phone and asked me where I was, I instinctively told him that I was home, in my bedroom. It might have been the first time I'd ever lied to him.

I was sitting in the shade of the water tower, studying for what would be my second pop quiz of the day, when I realized I wasn't alone. I could hear footsteps behind the water tower, circling around toward me. My body performed its standard panic routine: speeding heart, constricted throat, sweaty palms.

This is it, I thought, for the third or fourth time of the day. *This is how it ends.*

As usual, it was a false alarm. It was only Ashley.

"Seymour, hey," she said. "You made it."

"How did you get up here?" I demanded.

She shrugged.

"The stairs."

"What?" I said. "Are you *serious?*"

I started to gather up my stuff.

"They're probably coming up right now!"

She laughed.

"Oh, man," she said. "You better get out of here!"

I didn't know much about marijuana. Elliot never used it—he classified it as a "street drug"—and in fact, it was possible that I had never even seen it before. But I could tell that Ashley was pretty high.

"I come here every day," I told her, firmly. "I've been doing it for, like, six months."

"I've been coming longer than that," she said. "See? I have a chair."

She reached under the water tower and pulled out a folded red-and-white-striped lawn chair. It did look pretty old.

"You should get a chair," she said.

Ashley had spent the ninth and tenth grades away from Glendale. There were lots of rumors about where she had gone, and why, but no one knew any hard facts. Most people believed she had suffered some kind of breakdown, although some maintained that she had been impregnated by Han Wo, her foreign-exchange-student campaign manager, and had given birth to twins. What people did know is that when she returned, she was a completely different person. She'd lopped off her French braid and its absence was shocking, like she had returned to school an amputee. Her grades were awful, and she never, ever volunteered for anything. I liked to think Ashley had left Glendale for a number of reasons, and not just because of that ridiculous eighth-grade election. But of course I never asked her. I doubted that anyone had, not even her old friends from the math club. Ashley never even sat with anyone in the cafeteria. She just grabbed a plate of food and left—I guess, to come here.

"I saw you outside Lance's party on Saturday," she said. "You were pretending to talk on your cell phone. It was pretty crazy."

She shook her head and laughed.

"I mean, you looked like an actual crazy person."

"I have to go."

"Don't worry," she said. "No one saw. Except for me."

I reached for my notebook, but she snatched it up before I could get my hands on it.

"Give it back!" I shouted. I had meant the words to sound like an intimidating threat, but they came out as a childlike plea.

"Give it back," I repeated, in a deeper voice. Ashley was dangling my notebook over the side of the roof and humming some kind of off-key schoolyard taunt. Was she stoned enough to drop it? Would she use it to blackmail me into smoking her crazy drug? I didn't think the situation could get any worse—until she flipped the book around and started reading it.

"Pop quiz in English? Holy shit."

I started to stammer some kind of lie, but she didn't seem to be listening.

"Why are you cheating on this?" she asked.

"That's so hypocritical," I stammered. "I mean—you're doing *drugs.*"

She laughed.

"I'm not saying you shouldn't cheat," she said. "It just looks like a lot of work, is all. I mean it's just a *quiz.*"

She wiped her light-brown bangs away from her eyes and smiled at me.

"Do you need some help?" she asked. "Come on, I'll test you."

I grabbed the book out of her hand and crawled back into the steam vent.

"Good luck," she said.

• • •

Terry met me at the door in a riding jacket and boots.

"Welcome!" he said.

"Thanks," I said. "Did you have a nice time riding?"

"I haven't left the house in four days," he said. "Scone?"

"No thank you," I said. "Listen, I better go find Elliot. James came to my study hall and told me to come right after school."

"Elliot didn't send James," Terry said. "My son is having what can charitably be referred to as a 'bad day.' "

"Oh," I said.

There was a lull in the conversation; I heard a faint crashing noise in the distance.

"*I* sent James," Terry said, brightly. "Just because Elliot's feeling under the weather doesn't mean that we can't be sociable."

He grabbed me roughly by the elbow.

"Let's go to the study," he said. "I'll tell you an incredibly long story."

It was only half past three, but Terry's desk was already lined with decanters. The entire study was uncharacteristically disheveled—books on the floor, pillows strewn across the couch. The bear, I noticed, was wearing one of Terry's top hats.

"I should probably get going soon," I said. "I mean, if Elliot's sick."

"Nonsense!" Terry said. "Now, let's think . . . there must be one you haven't heard. Did I tell you about the time I spiked a '64 Bordeaux with GHB? So the editor of *Wine Spectator* looked drunk during his annual address?"

I nodded.

"What about my fortieth birthday party? Where I made all those rock bands reunite against their will?"

"You showed me the tape," I said.

"Did I tell you about what I did to that snooty literary magazine?"

"You mean when you bought an ad on every page? To turn it into a flip book?"

"Yes, but do you remember what *kind* of flipbook?"

"Was it . . . sexual?"

Terry sighed.

"You've heard all of my good ones."

I had never been in Terry's study this early in the day. It was strange to see it so brightly lit. Terry's leather chair looked almost red in the sun's glare and I could see flecks of dust swirling all over the room. Terry picked up a scone, looked at it for a moment, and then put it back in the basket. He leaned toward me.

"How is he?" he asked.

"Elliot? He's . . . well . . . I guess he's sick."

Terry took a handkerchief out of his pocket and blotted his bloated, red face. I felt a sudden urge to leave, but I had no idea how to do it politely.

"I know he's sick," he said. "What *else*?"

I remembered the note Terry had slipped into my birthday present back in the eighth grade. It had taken four years, but we were finally having the conversation he'd requested.

He looked me up and down, like he was trying to decide something.

"All right, Seymour," he said, finally. "Here's one you haven't heard."

• • •

"My wife, when I married her, was hilariously younger than I was. I won't use exact numbers. Let's just say that the age difference was so extreme, my priest refused to conduct the ceremony, even though my family had paid for the construction of his church.

"She was technically a princess, although she would blush and protest whenever anyone referred to her by her official title. I met her in Monte Carlo, at either a wedding or a funeral—I was too enraptured to focus on anything but her. There's a solid-gold statue of her in the Vatican, in the center of the holy courtyard.

Well, according to the plaque, it's the Virgin Mary. But the Pope instructed his sculptor to use my young wife as his model. She had the kind of face, you understand, that demanded simple worship.

"She had no real schooling, at least not in the academic sense. She was raised in a castle, you understand, by servants. She could play the harp, but she couldn't drive. She was fluent in Spanish, German, French, and English, but she counted on her fingers. Which was, of course, adorable. Her father was extremely old—she was his eleventh child. I offered to hire him a nursing staff when we got married, but she insisted he move in with us. She wanted to take care of the old man herself. By the time he arrived at our house, he had gone completely mad. He was a decorated World War II veteran—he had received the Croix de Guerre in 1939 while serving under Charles de Gaulle—and he believed the war was still in progress. He used to flip through the daily tabloids in disgust, furious that no one was covering the European conflict. When his delusions persisted, my wife called a house meeting and begged the servants not to contradict her father. If he asked for an update on the war, they were to say, 'The Russian army's closing in,' or, 'Hitler is on the run.' He always went berserk when he saw women wearing nylon, since the material was needed 'for the war effort.' So my wife banned stockings in the house. She also outlawed televisions, which my father-in-law found confusing. It was World War II in our home for that entire year, and on his deathbed, she told him we had won. She was that kind of woman.

"A few years after Elliot was born, she fainted on a cruise to Greece. She had gone up to the deck for some air, and if I hadn't taken to following her, who knows how long it would have been until someone discovered her. The ship's doctor, an incompetent, monkeylike idiot, prescribed aspirin. And the captain, trusting the medical man's expertise, refused to divert his course. I reasoned with him, threatened his life—but he wouldn't budge. In the end we settled on something like four hundred thousand dollars.

"We docked within an hour and took a cab to the closest hospital. My wife insisted she was feeling better, but I wasn't going to take any chances.

"It turned out she had kidney problems that had gone undiagnosed for some time. Every doctor I flew in agreed: She needed to find a donor, within weeks. The best specialist, a surgeon on Park Avenue, told me there was a shortage of transplants in the United States—and that my wife would have to go on some kind of government waiting list. I nodded and reached into my pocket, assuming he was signaling for a bribe. But apparently the list was real and somewhat ironclad.

"Within hours, James set me up with a prize-winning professor from Oxford, named Dr. Highsmith. He had been medical council to the Royal Family, among other nobility, until he had his license revoked for taking tips from his patients. I jetted out to England and handed him a single blank check.

"The doctor telephoned forty-eight hours later, from Thailand. He had found a Christian convent in the countryside. There were forty nuns, and all were in perfect health, thanks to a life of abstemious humility. Eight shared my wife's blood type, and four of those were sufficiently impoverished to sell a kidney. He compared and contrasted their vital statistics—their age, genetic histories, etc. But ultimately, he confessed, he couldn't determine the quality of their kidneys without removing them from their bodies and examining them directly. He couldn't tell me which nun to dissect.

"Until that moment, Dr. Highsmith had struck me as a particularly unsentimental man, a straight shooter whom I could see eye to eye with. But when I suggested he remove all four kidneys and pick the best one, he protested.

" 'What would you have me do with the remaining three?' he asked.

" 'Give them away,' I said, 'to some charity hospital.'

" 'We'd be caught instantly,' he said.

" 'Then I'll keep them on hand,' I said, 'in case my wife needs a spare.'

" 'They're not *sirloin steaks*,' he said. 'They don't "keep." '

" 'Then throw them in the garbage,' I said. 'Put them in a trash bag and throw them in the garbage can.'

"There was a long pause.

" 'Sir,' he said. 'Purchasing organs is already incredibly illegal, by any standard of the law. But to buy organs and *discard* them . . .'

"I thought about my lovely young wife, chatting with her old man about the advance of Stalin's army.

" 'I don't have time for this,' I said. 'Tell me within ten seconds.'

"I was about to hang up when I heard him clear his throat.

" 'Well, all right,' he said. 'But this is going to affect the fee.'

"And so we flew to Thailand. We bribed the proper officials, we purchased the correct equipment, we hired the right doctor and bought the right kidneys, we chose the best one and threw away the rest. And then she died anyway."

• • •

Terry relit his cigar and casually resumed smoking.

"That was a terrible story," he said. "I should have told you the one about the bear."

He gestured at the gigantic stuffed beast.

"That one's quite fun."

"How old was Elliot?" I asked. "When all of that happened?"

Terry shrugged.

"Who ever knows with that one?"

"He never told me that story," I said.

"He doesn't know it," Terry said. "I hope someday he'll think to ask."

He poured himself a large drink.

"I don't spy on him, you know," he said.

"What?"

"I could easily hire a spy," he said. "I have three full-time private investigators on retainer. I could have him tailed, but I don't. Not anymore. Because I don't care, Seymour. I couldn't care less. James writes me weekly reports—he's been doing it for years—and I throw them in the garbage. I throw them in the trash."

The sun had gone down, but Terry hadn't turned on any lights. I stood up and made my way across the darkened study.

"Stay!" he said. "Have a seat, have a brandy."

"It's getting pretty late," I said.

"I'll tell you about the bear," he said. "It's a good one!"

"I really need to—"

"It takes place at a circus and involves a professional fat lady."

"I shouldn't."

"It's sexual."

"I can't."

"Would you . . . like to see a painting? I'll show you a painting from my collection—something no one's ever seen before!"

"Mr. Allagash, I'm sorry, but I've got to go home. My parents are probably getting worried."

Terry blinked a few times and smiled broadly.

"Fine," he said. "That's just as well. That's fine."

I walked out into the hallway, my eyes burning at the brightness, and closed the heavy door behind me.

• • •

For as long as I could remember, my parents had been communicating with me through Post-it notes. They usually left me two or three bulletins a day, telling me who had called or where in the fridge I could find dinner. The notes were always a revealing indicator of what my parents thought of me. It wasn't what they wrote—they could only fit a few words onto those tiny yellow squares. It was where they placed them in the house. For instance, when I was in eighth grade, they posted all my Post-its on the Oreo cabinet, clearly determining that it was the one place in the apartment I was guaranteed to visit. At some point in high school, they had started tacking them to my bookshelf—convinced, evidently, that I had turned into a scholar. Lately, though, they had begun to plant the Post-its on my mirror.

> *Elliot called—×5*
> *Jessica called*

I ignored the top note and stared at the bottom one, convinced that I had misread it. How had Jessica even found my number? The class directory still listed the one from our old apartment. I peeled the Post-it off the mirror and held it up to the light. It felt irrationally substantial in my hands, as if her name had infused the paper with added mass.

I took out the directory, looked up her number, and dialed.

"Laura?" she asked.

"Um, no," I said. "It's Seymour?"

"Who?"

"Seymour?"

"Oh!"

"You called, right?"

"Oh, yeah! Mr. Hendricks gave me your number. He said, 'You need a tutor for the French test,' so I said, 'How about Seymour? He knows everything!' and he said, 'Okay,' so then I called you up!"

I covered up the receiver and cleared my throat.

"Can you believe how many tests there are?" I tried. "It's so *lame.*"

Jessica laughed. It was a miraculous sound, like coins falling out of a slot machine.

"Stop," she said, giggling. "Stop! Quit it!"

I heard some rustling, followed by some sharp squeals.

"Jessica?"

"Sorry," she said, panting. "Lance is being a jerk."

"Oh," I said.

"Are you free on Wednesday? Because the test is on—"

She squealed again—louder this time—and dropped the phone onto some kind of hard surface. I could hear both their voices now, but the sound was too muffled to make out any of the words. I felt like hanging up, but I didn't want to be rude. So I just sat there for a couple of minutes, waiting for them to finish whatever it was they were doing.

There's no way I could tutor Jessica—it would be a disaster. How could I teach her a language I didn't even speak?

Jessica sighed into the receiver.

"Sorry," she said.

"Listen, Jessica—I don't think I can."

"What?"

"Yeah, I'm just too busy."

"Okay, what about Tuesday?"

"No, I can't at all. I actually have to go."

"Oh, okay. Hey look, I'm sorry for bothering you! I just thought, you know, since you were good at French—"

"Yeah, it's okay. But I have to go now. Bye."

"Okay, bye—"

I closed my phone, shut the directory, and tossed the Post-it note into the garbage.

I should have known that's why she had called—what other reason could there possibly be? I pictured her in Mr. Hendricks's office, solemnly jotting down my phone number. And Lance doing God knows what while she reluctantly dialed it. But there was no time to think about all that—I had bigger problems. When Jessica told Mr. Hendricks I had refused to help her, he'd call me in for a meeting to ask why. I'd have to have some concrete alibi ready, so he wouldn't get any more suspicious than he was already. I took out my notebook and a pencil and called Elliot.

"Where were you?" he demanded. "I called your cell phone, your home phone, left messages on your voice mail and with your *mother* . . . I mean, *I* didn't actually physically do any of these things. James did, on my behalf. I've been in a custom-made bathing pool for the past four hours. But still, that's time James could have spent inventing me new cocktails."

"We have a problem," I said. "Jessica called and . . . she asked me to tutor her. I said no, but when Mr. Hendricks finds out—"

"Good God," Elliot interrupted. "*That's* why you're so addled?"

"I don't speak French, Elliot!"

He laughed.

"I take it from your tone that this has less to do with Hendricks than with Jessica."

"What are you talking about?"

"Give me some credit, Seymour. You thought, for a split second, that maybe she was calling because—"

"Elliot, this is serious, okay? My teachers are getting suspicious."

I made sure my door was locked and continued in a whisper.

"I'm not like *you*, okay? People actually care whether or not I'm lying to them."

Elliot scoffed.

"You think nobody keeps tabs on me? Come on. Terry thinks my attendance record at Glendale is 'stellar.' I have to bribe James every week to falsify his reports."

"It's different, though. I mean—your father doesn't even read those reports."

There was a pause.

"What do you mean?" he asked.

"He throws them away. He told me."

"When did he talk about me? What else did he say?"

"Do you really care?" I asked.

"Of course not!" he snapped. "I was just curious, but forget it."

There was a knock on my door.

"I have to go, Elliot—we're having dinner."

"Right now?"

"I'll talk to you some other time."

"Wait! Hold on—I'll help you with this Hendricks thing."

"Not now."

"I have a solution, but it's complicated—come over and we'll map it out."

"I can't. I got to go."

"You're going to want to hear this one, Seymour! I've been saving it—it's the perfect way to take him down!"

"Goodbye, Elliot."

"But—"

"Goodbye."

Figuring out the dynamics of the Allagash family was like try-ing to solve a complicated math problem: If Terry paid James x dollars to write him a weekly report about his son, and Elliot paid James y dollars to falsify that report, and Terry threw that report in the garbage, who came out ahead? How much would they save by simply talking to each other?

These are the questions I asked myself that night at dinner, as I ate with my parents in silence.

• • •

"I think this one is probably the most fucked up," Ashley said.

"Maybe," I said. "But it's useful research."

"It's a chart of Mr. Billings's shits."

"You said you'd help me," I said, grabbing my notebook out of her hands.

"I'll help, I'll help," she said. "But you have to tell me why you have this."

I pointed a finger at her.

"If you tell *anybody* about *any of this*—"

She laughed.

"I know, I know, you already threatened me."

"I shouldn't be talking to you at all," I said. "Honestly, I have no idea why we're even talking."

"Seymour, why would I tell on you?" she said. "I mean, who would even believe me?"

I hesitated.

"Okay. But *no interruptions.*"

I spread open the book and propped it up against the water tower.

"Mr. Billings is the high school registrar. That means he gets a copy of every final exam in advance."

"Really?"

"Yeah, so he can file them away for future reference. He also gets every student's report cards."

"Wow."

"I know. So obviously, it's important to know when he's going to be away from his office."

"So you can break into his desk."

I hesitated.

"Jesus, Seymour, relax!" she said. "There's nobody up here."

"Okay. Well . . . basically, there are two important things to know about him. The first is that he always eats lunch at twelve thirty. The second thing is that he has irritable bowel syndrome. Now usually after lunch, he goes straight to the fifth floor bathroom for about ten minutes. But on *these* days—"

I pointed to the calendar.

"He goes to the *eleventh-floor* bathroom. For over half an hour."

"Why?"

"I think because it's more remote. The eleventh floor is only accessible by Staircase B, and almost no one uses it. I guess he wants privacy for whatever goes on in there."

"No, I mean, why does it take him *so long* on those two days? What's special about them?"

"Oh," I said. "Well, that's when the cafeteria serves pizza."

She started to laugh out loud, getting louder and louder with every breath.

"Ashley!" I whispered. *"Shh!"*

She scrunched up her eyes and banged both fists against the water tower. I kept trying to shush her, but my pleas only seemed to make her laugh harder.

"What's so funny?" I demanded.

She tried to answer, but every time she caught her breath, the hysterics returned and she couldn't get any words out. Eventually, she grabbed my pencil and scribbled something onto my chart.

He eats the pizza <u>anyway!</u>

It *was* pretty amazing; Mr. Billings knew *exactly* what pizza did to him, but twice a month, he threw caution to the wind and went for it.

Ashley collapsed in her chair, spent. Her lips were parted and her chest was heaving. She eventually caught her breath. But when she opened her eyes and looked at me, it set her off again—and then we were both laughing, stomping our feet against the tar. She started shoving me and I grabbed both her wrists to make her stop. We tried to regain control of ourselves, but whenever we made eye contact, we started laughing again. When we were finally finished, I could feel an ache in my stomach, like I had just done a hundred sit-ups. There were tears in my eyes.

"Did Elliot think of that chart?" she asked, after we had caught our breath.

"Actually, that one was mostly my idea."

"Well it's pretty good," she said.

I blushed.

We ran through the answers to Douglas's history final until the ten-minute bell clanged softly in the distance.

"Do you want to hear something crazy?" I said, before heading down my tunnel. "It never occurred to me until now that there was something funny about that chart."

Ashley nodded solemnly.

"That *is* crazy," she said.

• • •

Elliot wheeled up the dumbwaiter and took out two items: a battered cell phone and a copy of the Yellow Pages. He flipped the book open to the Male Escorts section, grabbed the cell phone, and began to dial numbers. After about five calls, he put both objects back into the dumbwaiter and wheeled them down. Then he took out his Enemies book, unscrewed his pen, and made a little check mark.

"A waiter," he explained. "He tried to correct my pronunciation."

"Oh," I said.

Elliot took out a pink handkerchief and dramatically wiped his face. I could tell he wanted me to ask a follow-up question. "How did you get the waiter's cell phone?" for instance. Or, "How will those calls you made affect his life?" But I wasn't in the mood for a story.

It was my first trip to Elliot's house in nearly two weeks. I wasn't avoiding him, exactly. I just didn't need his help as much as I had before. It was hard work, perpetuating the strange identity that Elliot had constructed for me, but I had a handle on it. And besides, I wouldn't have to keep things up for much longer. There were only ninety-four days until college, where I would begin a new life as an anonymous freshman, free of my Glendale persona and all the pressure that came with it. As soon as I set foot on campus, I would put the past few years behind me and go back to being myself.

"Mr. Hendricks never said anything about the tutoring," I said. "So that's one thing we don't have to worry about."

Elliot ignored me.

"Steak tartare?" he said. "Clams Casino?"

I shook my head.

"James said you needed to tell me something? Something important?"

Elliot giggled.

The bags under his eyes had acquired a dark, bluish tint, and I could see the veins in his forehead, like strands of red thread.

"A new scheme," he said.

I shook my head.

"I don't have time."

"Okay," Elliot said.

I coughed, somewhat startled by his acquiescence.

"Okay," I said. "Then I guess . . . I'll see you later."

"I'll see you later," he said.

I grabbed my coat, buttoned up, and headed for the door.

"What was it?" I asked, suddenly curious.

"What was what?"

"The scheme?"

"Oh," Elliot said. "Nothing big."

"A school thing?"

"Nah," he said. "Just something with Jessica."

I stepped back inside.

"About . . . the tutoring thing?"

"No," Elliot said. "Unrelated."

He smirked.

"She's yours," he said. "If you want her."

I swallowed.

"What do you mean?"

"I think you know what I mean."

My heart was beating so fast, I felt like it might get dislocated. It was a sensation I hadn't experienced since the eighth grade, when Elliot had first shown up and offered me the world.

"What would I have to do?"

Elliot grinned.

"You should know by now," he said. *Everything I say.*"

• • •

I followed Elliot down the hall and into his creaky gated elevator. He jerked the hand crank and we lurched upstairs, to the very top floor of his ten-story home.

"I don't think I've ever been up here," I said.

"You haven't."

The gate swung open, revealing a long, narrow hallway. There were no lamps, but the moon shone brightly through skylights in the ceiling. The walls were lined with dozens of portraits. Some of the paintings were so old, the surfaces had cracked. I could tell by the clothes each figure wore that the paintings were arranged chronologically. And their proud smirks gave away that they were Allagashes.

I walked over to the first portrait, of an ancient, scowling king with a jet-black beard. He held a sword in his right hand; in his left, a bushel of grapes. A small bronze plaque listed the date as 1254.

"Is this the first Allagash?" I asked.

Elliot shook his head.

"It's fake," he said.

"You mean, this isn't a real portrait?"

"No," Elliot said. "This isn't a real person. None of these people existed."

He led me down the hall, past Renaissance and Victorian Allagashes.

"Terry had them all commissioned a few months ago. To trick some visiting countess into doing God knows what."

"Why did she care so much about his family?" I asked.

"Because she's a woman," Elliot said. "And women are easily confused. Jessica is no exception."

It was strange to hear Elliot refer to Jessica as a "woman." In my head, she was very much a girl. The only time I could remember using the word "woman" myself was in history class, when talking about the suffrage movement.

"Women's minds are often muddled," Elliot continued. "They think they're attracted to honor, or talent, or lineage, when in fact they're always attracted to the same thing: money."

We had sat down on a mahogany bench across from an armored medieval Allagash. He was bleeding from a wound in his chest and waving some kind of flag.

"I don't know, Elliot," I said. "There have to be *some* girls—or, you know, women—who care about other things. Besides money."

"Of course there are," he said. "Women value all sorts of commodities: fame, knowledge, glory, manners, looks, power, skill. But these are the lesser currencies of the world—the rubles, francs, and shekels! They can all be purchased with hard American cash."

He stared at me with an intensity that foretold a lengthy lecture.

"Women are on the same mental level as birds. They see shiny substances and they want them—but they're incapable of understanding why. Some women, for example, think they like diamonds. But diamonds are just rocks! Women are actually attracted to the money those diamonds are worth."

I thought, with some embarrassment, of my mom. My dad had given her a diamond necklace for one of her birthdays and her hands had shaken so much from the excitement that she needed help fastening the buckle.

"Women will refer to men as 'sophisticated,' or 'intelligent' or 'confident,' " Elliot said. "But they mean 'rich.' "

I thought about Lance. He was wealthy, but not as wealthy as some of the other guys in our class. Jessica liked Lance for other, more important reasons.

"What about being good at an instrument?" I said. "That's not something you can just *buy*. You have to be born with it."

Elliot smiled condescendingly.

"Ah," he said. "Talent!"

He stood up and began to pace.

"Lance was able to buy a guitar, an amplifier, and enough lessons to become proficient. His talent couldn't have cost his parents more than five thousand dollars. Think about the talent *I* could buy."

"What do you mean?"

"Lance is just a flash in the pan," he said. "Your album's going to be a critical and commercial sensation."

"What album?"

Elliot reached into his pocket and handed me a disc.

"I had James compose the tracks last night," he said. "It's called *The Seymour Herson Project*."

"Elliot, I don't even know any instruments!"

"I know," he said. "That's why I had no choice but to cast you as an experimental genius."

"What the hell does that mean?"

"The album's mostly sound effects. And spoken-word poetry."

"Oh my God," I said. "That sounds awful."

"The lyrics are in French."

"What? *Why?*"

"So no one can tell whether or not they're profound. If any-one asks what they mean, by the way, you're to say they're 'existen-tial.' "

He shook his head.

"It's pathetic we have to stoop to this," he muttered. "In an-cient Rome, the only people who played music were *slaves*—and emperors who had gone mad."

"Elliot, I *really* don't think this is going to work. I mean, who would want to listen to music like this?"

Elliot rolled his eyes.

"If Joe Kennedy could make his syphilitic son a bestselling au-thor and then president of the United States, I think I can turn you into some avant-garde artist."

I laid the disc down on the bench.

"I don't think I want to do this," I said. "It's too much. The school stuff is fine . . . I'm going to be out of there soon. But this is the kind of thing that could really screw up my life."

"Two things," Elliot said. "One: It's too late. I've already mass-mailed your demo to every trendsetter in Williamsburg."

"Oh my God."

"Two: It's going to work."

He opened the elevator gate and yanked me inside.

"Do you trust me?"

I didn't respond.

"Seymour, everything I've ever done has been to your advantage."

He leaned in so close that our faces were practically touching.

"Do you trust me or not?"

I nodded slightly.

"All right," he said, catching his breath. "Okay."

He jerked on the hand crank and the elevator went into motion.

"Going down."

• • •

I hurried silently through my living room, narrowly avoiding eye contact with my parents. Then I locked my door, put on my headphones, and fearfully slid Elliot's disc into my stereo.

I had known Elliot Allagash for more than four years. I was still as frightened of him as ever. But I liked to think I had grown used to him, that he had lost the ability to shock me. I liked to think I had already seen his madness at its worst.

I took a deep breath and pressed play.

The Seymour Herson Project began with a lengthy stretch of ambient sound. About forty seconds in, a siren started wailing, accompanied by gunshots. These noises were interrupted by the sound of a child laughing and, for some reason, the melody of "The Star-Spangled Banner." Eventually, a computerized voice took over, reciting a lightning fast monologue in French. The song, according to the track listing, was called "Rape."

The demo was humiliating. But when I took off the headphones, I actually felt somewhat relieved. It didn't matter how many demos Elliot sent out; there was no way music that ridiculous could find listeners. Jessica would never learn of its existence, Elliot would forget about the scheme, and life would go back to some semblance of normalcy.

By this point, I really should have known better.

• • •

"I heard your song on the radio," Lance said. "It's pretty cool, I guess."

"He didn't get that it was an allegory," Jessica said.

"Yes I did," Lance said, glaring at her. "I was about to say that's what it was, before that critic guy jumped in."

"*Sure,*" Jessica said.

Lance clenched his jaw and shuffled out of the cafeteria.

"He didn't get it," Jessica said, smiling mischievously at me. "But I did."

She was wearing dangerously low-hanging sweatpants. I tried not to stare as she pulled up her waistband, barely concealing the grooves of her hip bones.

"The guy on the radio said the song was existential," she said. "Is that true?"

There was a fairly long pause.

"Yes," I said, finally.

Jessica pursed her lips and nodded, as if reflecting upon my response.

"Well I better go," she said, rolling her eyes in Lance's direction.

There was a Glendale lion stitched onto her upper thigh. And when she walked away, I noticed that the word ROAR was emblazoned on the seat of her pants, two letters per buttock.

It was probably a good time to call Elliot.

I took a deep breath, dialed him up and addressed him as calmly as I could.

"What the fuck is going on?" I said. "Tell me what the fuck is going on."

"Relax," he said. "It's just a college radio show! I bribed a local DJ."

"Jessica and Lance *heard* it!"

"Of course they did. You took Lance's regular slot."

"This is insane! Jessica thinks I'm some kind of *artist*. What the hell am I supposed to do now?"

Elliot laughed.

"I don't know, Casanova. *You're* the one who ordered her. I'm just the delivery man."

I sat down on a stoop.

"I guess James could give you some pointers," he said, "if you're really lost in that department."

"I have to go."

"Seymour, I must say! You sound less *exhilarated* than I would expect, given the circumstances. Isn't this something you wanted?"

"Yes! But—it's just happening a little *fast*."

"Fast? You've been chasing this nymphet for the better part of a decade. And now, just as she's about to pay dividends, you're ready to *sell*?"

"That's not it," I said. "I just feel weird about this whole thing."

Elliot sighed heavily.

"Terry and I flew to China five years ago," he said, "because they were about to outlaw the consumption of monkey brains. We drove straight from the airstrip to the Manchu Imperial and ordered a king-size portion. But when they placed the giant, screaming monkey in the center of the table and started to peel back his scalp, Terry lost his appetite. You haven't lost your appetite, have you, Seymour? Because monkey brains are expensive."

"I have to go," I said.

"Seymour—"

"I have to *go.*"

I shut my phone and walked four laps around the block. What the hell was wrong with me? Elliot was absolutely right—I should be feeling ecstatic. But the only emotion I could identify was a vague and pressing dread.

For the first time in years, I found myself thinking about video games.

Before I met Elliot, I owned a game called Ninja Streets. The game followed the adventures of Mack, a mustachioed vigilante, as he made his way through a city that, for reasons unknown, had become positively *overrun* with ninjas. It wasn't a challenging game. The ninjas always screamed as they approached, which took away any element of surprise. And they only attacked from the right side of the screen, so you never had to move. My strategy was to punch the air and wait for the ninjas to walk into my moving fist.

Ninja Streets was more an endurance test than anything else. The ninjas Mack faced weren't talented; they were just numerous. Each level contained 128 ninjas. And if you stopped punching the air for even two seconds—to respond to one of your mother's questions about dinner, say, or take off your sweatshirt—you were finished.

According to a chat room I frequented at the time, Ninja Streets had 256 levels. All the levels were identical, except for the last one. Apparently, if you somehow made it to level 256, the game broke down. No one in the chat room could tell me what this breakdown entailed, but everyone insisted it was real.

I often daydreamed about what it would be like to reach the end of Ninja Streets. (Would Mack run for mayor? Would he leave the city and move to a more reasonable community?) But I knew that victory was impossible. I had played the game every day for months and I had never even gotten to level 100 without losing focus. One day, though, I read an online post, and everything changed.

Ninja Streets Unlimited Health: Up-Down-Back-Right-B-A-Select

Suddenly, anything was possible.

I took out a pencil and did some calculations. Each level had a ten-minute time limit. But it never took more than two and a half minutes to defeat each batch of ninjas. If I played continuously, without pausing for food or drink, I could get to the final ninja street in just under eleven hours.

The next morning, I faked a cold, cracked a fresh box of Oreos, and went to work. It was a grueling day, and I often lost concentration—but it didn't matter. I was now impervious to my enemies' blows. At one point, to break the monotony, I decided to take a break from punching. A ninja screamed, then entered. After a brief pause, he tentatively began to punch me in the face. When he realized I wasn't interested in retaliating, he worked up the nerve to do his special move: a jump kick to the face. When I didn't respond to this aggression, either, he began to walk back and forth across the screen, as if in contemplation. I eventually punched him in the face and moved on to the next enemy.

I got to level 256 just before bedtime. It started off completely normal—and for a terrifying moment, I thought I'd been had. But then it happened. About thirty ninjas into the level, the right half of the screen turned black. The left side of the street was still intact, and the music still played aggressively in the background. But there were no more ninjas coming and there was nowhere left to go.

I watched in disbelief as the clock began to wind down. Seven minutes passed, then eight, then nine. I jammed the arrow forward with all my strength, but all I could do was run in place in the center of the screen, my face pressed up against the blackness. At the moment time ran out, Mack turned, as if to face me. His fists were raised to the heavens, and his eyes were wide with horror. He froze in that pose, at the edge of the void, then vanished.

Game over.

• • •

Ashley took a carton of chocolate milk out of her backpack and poured it into a ceramic kettle.

"Hot chocolate?"

"It's okay," I said. "You can have it."

"I don't want any."

"Really? Well, then, okay. Thanks."

She reached under the water tower and placed the kettle on an exposed metal heating pipe. We had been meeting on the roof every day for weeks but had only recently learned how to make hot chocolate. Like all great discoveries, it had been an accident. I had touched the pipe by mistake while reaching for a fallen pencil and singed a couple of my fingers. I probably would have started sobbing if Ashley hadn't been there to examine the burn and pronounce it "no big deal." A few seconds later she was crawling under the water tower, her face dangerously close to the pipe. "Hey, buddy!" she said. "We can make hot chocolate!"

We sat for a few minutes in silence, waiting for the milk to heat.

"That song is horrible," she said. "Someone played it for me in the hallway. Was it really on the radio?"

I nodded.

"How did that happen?"

"Elliot."

She poured the warm milk into a mug and handed it to me.

"Are you going to have to be a rock star now?" she asked.

"I don't know," I said. "I really don't know."

I took a long sip. It was an overcast day, and we could see a woman selling umbrellas on the sidewalk. When people walked by her table, she pointed dramatically at the sky and shouted. But everyone ignored her.

"Remember that party at Lance's?" she said. "When you pretended to talk on your phone?"

Some blood rushed to my cheeks.

"What about it?"

"I didn't go either," she said. "I mean, I *went*. To the street. But

I stayed outside the whole time. That's why I was sure no one saw you. Because I was watching from behind the next tree."

"Really?"

"Yeah," she said. "It was so stupid. Like middle school."

A bolt of lightning zigzagged in the distance, followed by a lazy growl of thunder.

"When I was in the hospital," she said, "I met someone who thought he controlled the weather."

I nodded as casually as I could. It was the first time I'd heard Ashley talk about being in a hospital.

"His name was King Elijah," she said. "I think he was from Scarsdale. He was short and sort of chubby, with acne."

"Why did he think he controlled the weather?"

"It had to do with visions he was receiving in his dreams. He'd get messages from God, or the Devil, and then he'd have to decode them using algebra. It was really complicated. He was always asking to borrow my calculator. After a few hours, he'd be left with some incantations—which he could use to manipulate the sun."

"Oh."

"He always tried to get us good weather, but it rained that whole winter. He was always so guilty about it. I told him I didn't mind, that I liked the rain. But he could tell I was lying and that I was just trying to make him feel better."

"What happened?"

"It was wild: Another god moved into the facility. Some kid from Long Island named Cronos."

"Cronos?"

"Well, his real name was Ben—but he did *not* like it when you called him that. He also controlled the weather, but he didn't need to do any calculations like King Elijah. He could just make stuff happen with his mind. Earthquakes, tsunamis, pretty much anything."

"Were they friends?"

"No," she said. "They did *not* get along."

"I guess that makes sense."

"Yeah. It was especially awkward during group. Eventually though, King Elijah stopped working so hard on his calculations. After a few weeks, he became convinced that Cronos was more powerful than he was. And that it was pointless to manipulate the sun, because Cronos could just overrule him. He stopped asking for my calculator and apologizing for all the rain. And a few weeks after that, he was gone."

She looked up at the clouds and squinted; it had started to drizzle.

"I bet King Elijah's doing better by now. But Cronos is probably still in there."

She looked at me.

"No one should have to control the weather."

She stood there, waiting for me to respond. It was so silent, I could hear both of us breathing.

The bell rang harshly in the distance, and I quickly packed up my books.

"I'm sorry," I said, handing her my almost-full mug. "I've got to go."

She didn't respond.

"I'll see you tomorrow—fifth period."

I hopped over the heating pipe and started to squeeze into my tunnel.

"You don't have to," she said. "It's not required."

"What?"

"You don't have to come at all," she said. "I'm not keeping attendance."

"Ashley—"

"I tell you about a serious thing, something I've never told *anyone* about, and you just get up and go back to your stupid quizzes."

"Ashley, come on."

"Why do I even talk to you? I mean, you'd rather go down a *tunnel* than be seen walking around with me!"

"Ashley, it's not that; there's a camera behind the door—"

"We never hang out in school."

"Well what do you want me to do? I've got a reputation to maintain! I can't just walk around constantly with someone like—"

I stopped myself, but it was obviously too late. Ashley tilted her head down and looked away. The rain picked up suddenly, but she didn't budge. A few wet strands of hair fell over her eyes. Her arms glistened with rain. I stayed there for a moment, with my head poking out of the tunnel.

"Ashley—"

"You better go," she said. "You don't want to be late."

• • •

Elliot sat by the dumbwaiter, a phone in each hand.

"Next month in Paris," he said into one of them.

"Save a bottle for me!" he said into the other.

He snapped both phones shut simultaneously and sighed wearily.

Usually, when I entered the billiards room, Elliot was in the process of hanging up on someone. Two phones were not unusual—and there were sometimes as many as four laid out by his drink. Standing there that day, some unsettling questions occurred to me for the first time: Who was he always hanging up on? Why did they always seem to bother him the moment before my arrival? Were there really people on the other lines?

"My apologies," Elliot said. "I've been meaning to prune my correspondences."

I nodded.

"But on to the news of the day!" he said. "You're going to be on *television*. It's a live production called *Little Miracles*. Some mindless talk show, to sell garbage to women."

I had seen *Little Miracles* a couple of times while home sick. They filmed it every afternoon in a studio in Times Square. There was a live studio audience and glass walls, so people on the street could hold up signs and be on television.

"Elliot, that's insane. I mean, what do they even want me to do?"

"You won't have to *do* anything, Seymour. Just a couple of scripted banalities and you'll be on your way. It's tomorrow during your free period. James will drive."

"You mean fifth period?"

"Yes."

I thought about Ashley, sitting alone by the water tower, heating hot chocolate and watching the mouth of the steam tunnel.

"I don't think I can go," I said.

Elliot sighed angrily.

"Tell me why."

"I have to be somewhere," I said.

"*Have* to?"

"Or, you know . . . I *want* to. I want to be somewhere."

Elliot clenched his jaw.

"Where? *Where could you possibly have to be?*"

His fists were trembling. He took a deep breath and shook them out.

"I'm sorry," he said. "I forget sometimes how much spelling-out your mind requires. That I need to you address you as I would a small child."

He poured himself a glass of Scotch from a crystal decanter.

"Women *watch* these shows. Their opinions, or the recycled pap they consider to be their opinions, *originate* on them."

"So what?"

"So. Every woman from Glendale will tune in to see you. *Including* Jessica. Do you want her or not?"

I hesitated.

"I don't know."

"You don't know."

He finished his drink and poured a second, spilling some Scotch over the sides of his glass.

"You know, Seymour, if you wanted that mousy Ashley girl, you could have just said something. I could have had her for you by now, and it would have been a whole lot cheaper."

I froze. How did he know about Ashley?

"We're just friends."

Elliot laughed.

"You're *what?*"

"Friends."

Elliot clapped his hands.

"A social alliance with a mental patient. That's your new strategy!"

"It's not a *strategy,* Elliot. Not everything is a strategy."

"Oh yeah? Why do you think she's even talking to you? To hear your brilliant *bons mots*? She's trying to get her claws into you, so you can drag her up from the ocean floor."

"Elliot—"

"Falling for a woman is one thing, but Ashley! Christ! That's like a gold miner happening upon some quartz and—"

"Elliot, just shut up."

"All right, all right, good Lord! If you're going to be this *irrational,* I'll get her for you! We'll start planning it out right now."

"No."

Elliot froze for a moment and then forced a chuckle.

"Of course," he said. "You don't need my help for something so trivial. We'll move on to something else."

He started in on some new idea—but I interrupted him.

"It's not that I don't need you to help," I said. "It's that I don't think you *could.*"

Elliot stared at me, nostrils flaring.

"Excuse me?"

"If I wanted to be with Ashley . . . you wouldn't know how to help me with that. You would be totally lost."

Elliot's eyes narrowed.

"Do me a favor, Seymour: Don't tell me that I don't know how a thing works."

"You don't know how *this* works, Elliot. You haven't the slightest idea. I mean, how would you? You've never had a friend in your whole life."

Elliot turned away from me, and I could see his bony shoulders heaving. When he turned back around, his face was flushed and wrinkled. For a moment, it almost looked like he was crying.

"Elliot," I said. "Listen—"

He picked up his decanter and hurled it against the pool table. It shattered, spilling glass and Scotch across the felt.

"Out!" he screeched. "Out!"

I ran into the hallway, slamming the door just before a billiard ball collided with it.

"I can take it back!" he shouted, hurling another ball against the door. "All of it!"

I sprinted down the staircase, my damp palms slipping on the banister.

"All I have to do is snap! That's all it takes!"

I could hear Elliot behind me, screaming hysterically at the top of the stairs.

"You're just a hobby! A mouse I've been playing with! And now I'm through playing! I'm finished! I'm *through*!"

I ran through the lobby and pushed open the door. The storm had gotten worse. I paused at the threshold for a moment, catching my breath, staring at a wall of rain.

And then I ran home.

• • •

My dearest Seymour,

Congratulations! You are the proud recipient of an Allagash Apology. I suggest you frame and mount it—you'll probably never see one again!

I feel just awful about our encounter the other night. We both said some rather harsh things, and I sincerely hope we can get past them. I've been severely sleep-deprived this week, and I would hate for you to misconstrue a physiological symptom for genuine animosity.

I promise to stop meddling in your affairs. You've grown into an inspiring individual, and you don't need my help. The truth is that you never really did.

Sincerely,
Elliot

P.S. I've tried to cancel your appearance on that foolish television show, but I guess you were right about my general ineptitude. They won't take no for an answer! You're a star, Seymour, whether you like it or not. I'll be watching you at home, rooting as always.

I sat at the foot of my bed and took out my notebook. In just a couple of weeks, my time at Glendale would finally be over, and I'd be able to incinerate the entire sordid volume. Feeling nostalgic, I flipped back to the very first page:

HENDRICKS POP QUIZ—4/18, 2:45PM—"THE SHOPS OF FRANCE"

1) C
2) A
3) B
4) D
5) B

EXTRA CREDIT: MR. HENDRICKS'S COLLEGE A CAPELLA GROUP WAS CALLED THE FUNKTONES.

I skipped to the last page of the book and wrote down my last few reminders.

LITTLE MIRACLES TV INTERVIEW—5/28, 1:30 PM
1) MEET JAMES IN LOBBY DURING FIFTH PERIOD
2) LYRICS TO MY SONGS ARE "EXISTENTIAL"

It was a relief when I found Elliot's wax-sealed letter, planted (somehow) inside my locker. I *had* said some cruel things. And even though I was glad to have stuck up for myself, I couldn't help but feel guilty about what I'd said. Still, I must have been somewhat in the right; otherwise, there's no way Elliot would have forgiven me. There was a new tone in his note, something almost like respect.

My mother knocked softly on my door.

"Seymour? If you're hungry, there's dinner."

"Okay."

"Are you going to join us?" she asked.

"Just give me a minute," I said.

I flipped through the pages, marveling at the volume of frenzied, scribbled text.

"I'm almost done."

• • •

I was standing by my locker, trying to smooth the knot in my necktie, when Jessica sidled up next to me.

"I heard you're going to be on TV," she said. "Is it true?"

"Who told you that?"

"I don't remember," she said. "It's going around."

I nodded. Elliot had probably leaked the rumor on my behalf.

"What are you going on for?" she asked.

What was I going on for. It was a good question. If I was going to live more independently and rely less on Elliot's influence, why not start now? I pictured James waiting downstairs, robotically scanning the lobby for my face. And I pictured Ashley on the roof, checking her watch and waiting for the bell. I still hadn't apologized to her. Wasn't the choice obvious?

"I think it's pretty cool," Jessica said. "I mean, *television*."

She arched her back against my locker and the bottom of her shirt inched up, revealing her bejeweled belly button. I was putting a book away and her light-brown hair fell gently over my fingers.

"It's exciting," she said.

"Oh . . . well . . . you know. It's no big deal."

Ashley wouldn't care if I skipped one day. I could apologize some other time. I smiled at Jessica and headed for the lobby.

"Break a leg," she said.

• • •

Little Miracles was hosted by a married couple named Mike and Suzie. It had started as a segment at the end of the news but had gotten so popular that eventually the network had no choice but to make a full show of it. The first segment was usually devoted to a person who had accomplished something unusual, like a housewife who had invented a new kind of sponge, or an old person who had climbed a mountain. In the second segment, Mike and Suzie found somebody who was poor or sick and gave them something they needed in order to survive, like expensive medicine, or a new roof for their house. In the last segment, they gave stuff away to the audience. It was usually makeup, since their sponsor was a cosmetics company (owned, of course, by Allagash Industries).

I had never been interviewed before, for any reason. But I wasn't particularly nervous. If I could handle four years of Elliot Allagash, I reasoned, I could handle thirty minutes of anything.

• • •

It was the first time I had ever ridden in Elliot's limo without Elliot. I was proud that I had stood my ground and convinced him to keep his distance. But it felt awkward to ride alone with James. The truth was, in four years we had never actually had a real conversation. Halfway to Times Square, I decided to reach out. After all, it could be my last chance.

"Must be a pretty fun job," I said, "traveling around with the Allagashes."

James didn't respond, but he looked at me in the rearview mirror. His eyes were craterous, black, dead. I decided not to ask him any more questions.

When we got to the studio he stated my name to a woman with a clipboard. I tried to thank him for driving me, but by the time I turned around he was gone.

The lady led me into a small, green room and sat me down in front of a mirror, framed with light bulbs. There was a gigantic fruit basket on the table, with a card stapled to it that read SEYMOUR HERSON. I hadn't had lunch yet, and I was about to unwrap the cellophane when another woman came in to put makeup on my face.

"Don't eat anything," she said, when she was finished dabbing me with powder. "You'll mess it up."

Both women left, and I sat for a while staring at the fruit and nuts and chocolate.

There was a knock on the door, and Mike strolled into the room. He was wearing a bib and his face was caked with a layer of pink makeup.

"Don't you fucking tell me this," he said. "Don't you fucking dare."

I panicked for a moment, until I realized that he was talking into a headset phone.

"Sorry," he whispered to me. "I have to deal with this."

He looked older than he did on television, and his voice wasn't as gentle.

"Fuck you," he was saying. "No, no—you can't book another retard. We've already had two this month."

He rolled his eyes at me apologetically.

"Down's? Light or full-blown? Okay, fine."

He took off his phone and removed a stack of note cards from his pocket.

"Seymour Herstein!" he said.

"Herson," I said.

"Fine," he said. "So, I give a signal, you come out, we ask a few questions, and you answer them. It doesn't matter what you say—Suzie's going to interrupt anyway. But you have to smile. You got that? Here, let me see you smile."

I smiled.

He leaned back and squinted at me for a moment.

"Okay," he said. "Fine. Just keep doing that until the charity segment. When that starts, make sure to frown. Like this."

He frowned.

"Who's coming out after me?" I asked.

"Some French guy with heart problems."

"What's his name?"

He shrugged.

"I should really have learned it by now. He's on all the time."

"Really?"

"Yeah, they keep patching him up, and he keeps falling apart. We've gotten nine segments out of him in three years. He's the gift that keeps on giving. Here, let me see your frown."

I frowned.

"Not bad. Okay, then you smile again at the end, during the makeup giveaway. So it's smile, frown, smile. Got it?"

I nodded awkwardly.

"Holy shit," he said, flipping through his note cards. "You're some ambitious kid!"

He laughed.

"Well, congratulations," he said. "You made it."

• • •

The studio was smaller than I had pictured—just five or ten rows of seats. And when the woman with the clipboard took me backstage, I actually felt relieved. The Glendale auditorium had more than forty rows, plus a balcony, and I had been on that stage plenty of times.

But then I noticed the cameras. There were three of them: one on the left, one on the right, and one in the middle. They were all aimed at the stage, like three monstrous eyes.

"Our first guest is a painter, musician and amateur scientist . . ."

In commercials for *Little Miracles,* the announcer said, "Find out why a million New Yorkers wake up each day with Mike and Suzie." A million New Yorkers. That was a lot of people.

202 • ELLIOT ALLAGASH

"... a *linguist,* a community *activist*..."

If the Knicks sold out Madison Square Garden, it meant 20,000 New Yorkers had shown up to the arena. Going onstage would be like visiting *fifty* Madison Square Gardens, each one packed to the brim.

"... and he's not even old enough to vote!"

The lady with the clipboard shoved me on the shoulder, and I wandered out onto the stage. The lights were so bright, I couldn't see the audience.

Suzie shook my hand and handed me a coffee mug filled with water. She was wearing so much makeup it looked like a mask of clay and her teeth were the color of bone. Mike came over and patted me on the back, grinning broadly at the audience.

"Smile," he whispered, through gritted teeth.

I smiled.

Mike started to ask me questions about all of the things I had supposedly accomplished. I didn't really know how to respond to most of them, but luckily, Suzie did most of the talking. At one point, Mike asked me why I wrote my lyrics in French, and I mumbled something about existentialism. I was terrified that Mike would ask me a follow-up question, like, "What is existentialism?" but after a brief pause, Suzie stood up and pointed at me.

"Do you have a date to the *prom?*"

The audience burst into laughter, and Mike cut away to a commercial.

I couldn't believe it: It was over. I stood up excitedly, but Mike clamped his hand on my shoulder.

"Where are you going, kid? There are still two segments left."

I sat back down.

"Existentialism," he said. "My God. You must be rolling in high school pussy."

He glared at Suzie with undisguised revulsion. Her eyes were closed, and two old men were dabbing at her face with cotton balls.

"Enjoy it while it lasts," he said.

He turned toward the camera, grinning just before it clicked back on.

Suzie introduced the next guest and an elderly man walked out onto the stage. She described his heart condition, and it sounded horrible. He'd had nine operations and none of them had fully solved the problem. He still had attacks all the time, Suzie said, and if he didn't take a pill right away, he would die. These pills were expensive, though, and he couldn't afford to pay for them much longer. Mike handed him a novelty-sized check—enough for a lifetime supply of heart pills—and the audience applauded. The old man said something in French and Suzie made a joke about how she should have studied harder in high school. The audience laughed and Mike cut away to another commercial. There was only one segment left.

The French guy sat down next to me on the couch, awkwardly avoiding eye contact. His scalp was bald and spotted, and his face was almost cartoonishly wrinkled. For the first time all day, I felt truly guilty. For me, this TV appearance was a lark. For him, it was a matter of life and death. They'd shown footage of him and his wife walking hand in hand across their vineyard. His heart condition had made it impossible for him to work more than an hour or two a day, and they would almost definitely have to sell their patch of land. We sat in silence as a couple of workers wheeled a mound of eyeliner pencils onto the stage.

The few times I had seen *Little Miracles,* I had been amazed by how excited the audience got during the third segment. Mike and Suzie gave away lipstick or mascara at the end of every single episode. But when Mike finished dealing with the needy person and Suzie unveiled that giant stack of merchandise, the crowd always lost it. Suzie would try to talk about the product—its softness, its smoothness—but you could barely hear her over the sounds of women screaming. Eventually, when Suzie was finished describing the product, Mike would give some kind of signal and the women would rush the stage, grabbing at the pile with both hands until it was gone.

If that's how they responded to makeup, you can imagine how they'd react if something *truly* shocking were to happen.

Suzie started reading her lines off of the teleprompter, but before she had finished the first sentence, I heard a loud gasp. I looked over—and the French man was clutching the table with both hands.

"It's his heart!" someone shouted. "He needs his pills!"

A woman in the audience screamed, and all of the cameramen started shouting into their walkie-talkies.

"Where are your pills?" Mike shouted. "Where are they?"

The old man grabbed Mike's note card, scribbled something down and handed it back to him. Mike stared at it in horror.

"It's French!"

Suzie pointed at me from across the room.

"Seymour! Seymour can translate!"

Mike handed me the card as the three cameras swiveled toward me.

"Kid, what's he saying?"

The studio went silent as I looked down at the card. The old man had printed a few French words, underlining each one for emphasis. They were meaningless to me.

"Damn it, Seymour!" Mike shouted. "What does it say?"

The old man grabbed his heart, let out a scream, and collapsed onto the pile of eyeliners. The makeup scattered noisily across the stage.

"Does anybody speak French?" I shouted.

"Don't *you*?" Suzie said.

I looked up at the camera, still holding the card in my hands.

"Jesus, kid," Mike said, shaking his head in disgust. *"Jesus."*

The audience fled the studio as the old man writhed in agony on the ground. His arms were shaking spastically at his sides, but as soon as the cameraman yelled, "Cut," they stopped. I took a step toward him. Somehow, his eyes looked familiar.

"Oh my God," I whispered. *"James?"*

He pressed a single finger to his lips.

"Jesus Christ!" I shouted.

He hopped to his feet and brushed himself off. The studio was so panicked, no one seemed to notice he had stood up. I could hear a siren in the distance. He took out his cell phone and pressed a single button.

"It's done," he said.

"Wait!" I said. "James—you need to explain this to the ambulance! People are going to think I—"

He clamped his hand over my mouth and leaned in close. His breath was foul and his makeup had cracked from perspiration. It was shocking; Elliot had trained me, coached me, fought for me for years. Had he held this card the entire time, just in case?

"It's over," James said. "You can go."

"How could you do this to me?" I demanded.

He sighed wearily.

"Trust me, kid," he said. "You owe me a thank-you."

• • •

I wandered out of the studio and back to school, but I couldn't bring myself to enter the building. I could see people I knew in the lobby, talking, laughing, slapping hands. They probably didn't know about the fiasco yet, but it was only a matter of time. The entire world had ended and I was the only one who knew about it. Without even noticing what I was doing, I took out my cell phone and dialed Elliot's number. It rang twice before I realized he wasn't going to answer. I pictured him sitting in his billiards room, adding my name to his Enemies book. Had he made his check mark yet? Or was he just getting started?

"Hey!"

I let out a frightened gasp. Jessica was standing by the bicycle rack, smoking a cigarette.

"I taped it," she said. "We're all going to watch it after school. Me, Lindsay, Tamara . . ."

I nodded automatically as she recited more names, each one landing like a violent blow to the face. What were these people going to do to me when they found out I was a fraud?

"Are you okay?" she said.

"I'm fine," I said.

"You just seem—"

"I'm *fine.*"

"You know, I've been thinking about your song a lot, and I was wondering, like—"

"I don't want to talk about it."

She threw down her cigarette.

"I'm not stupid, you know," she said.

"What?"

"I'm not stupid!"

She looked away, embarrassed.

"Okay, fine, I don't get the song! But that's because no one will explain it to me! People think, 'What's the point, she won't get it.' Well maybe I would if they explained it to me!"

She looked down at her feet, blinking rapidly. I couldn't believe it: She was crying.

"I've listened to that awful song a hundred times," she said. "And when I try to talk about it, people laugh! Do you know what that's *like?*"

For the first time, I thought about what Jessica must think of me. I never came to parties or said a kind word to anybody. Everything I did or said was more or less calculated to make her feel inferior.

"Jessica—"

"What?"

"I don't get it, either."

She looked up.

"What?"

"That song, the one they played on the radio . . . I didn't write it. It was somebody else. I have *no idea* what it means."

She wiped her face, smudging her makeup a little.

"Really?"

"Yeah," I said. "And you know what else? The person who wrote it doesn't know what it means, either! So if people say you don't get it, they're the ones who are stupid—because there's nothing to *get*. The song is nonsense!"

"That's what I thought," she whispered. "I didn't tell anyone, but that's what I always thought!"

"Well, you were right," I said.

She laughed for a moment and then stifled it, covering her mouth with her hands. She looked over her shoulder and then smiled at me conspiratorially.

"I won't tell," she said. "I promise."

"It's okay," I said. "It doesn't matter. You can tell whoever you want."

She hesitated.

"Can I tell Lance? He'll be so happy—he didn't get the song either!"

"Yeah," I said. "Tell Lance."

"Seymour . . . what's going on with you?"

I sighed.

"I'm in trouble, Jessica."

Her eyes widened with genuine concern.

"Big trouble?"

"I think so."

She flashed me a friendly smile.

"It'll be okay, Seymour," she said. "I mean, how bad could it be?"

RETRACTIONS

The New York Times

An article published on October 15, "High School Activist Skips Prom to Fight Disease," contained several errors.

• The article's subject, Seymour Herson, was referred to as Secretary of the Anti-Asbestos League of New York. He does not hold that position. In fact, no such organization exists.

• The article erroneously stated that Seymour was attempting to cure Pasternak-Schwarzschild's disease. He has never attempted to cure this disease.

• The article reported that Seymour speaks four languages. In fact, he speaks only one language, English.

• The article erroneously reported that Seymour Herson's favorite book is *Gravity's Rainbow,* by Thomas Pynchon. Seymour Herson has not read this book.

• The article contained an anecdote, which was supplied to the Times by a "close friend," in which Seymour visited a museum. In the anecdote, Seymour became so absorbed in a Cezanne painting that when a guard told him the museum was closing, he failed to hear him, and had to be "physically shaken." This event did not take place.

• It was reported that Seymour Herson had to choose between laboratory research and attending the Glendale Senior Prom "with a date." Seymour did not in fact have a date to this prom.

The Times regrets the errors.

Art in America

Our annual painting roundup misattributed a painting, *Green Waters,* to the artist Seymour Herson. In fact, the painting is the work of Terry Allagash. The legendary tycoon says he painted the work under a pseudonym in order to "receive fair evaluation from critics."

Art in America congratulates Mr. Allagash on his major achievement.

Bishop House Fall Books Catalogue

The editors of Bishop House would like to announce the following changes to our publication schedule.

Marxian Semiotics, the third work by Professor Daniel Herson of Fordham University, will no longer be released this fall. The book has been canceled and Professor Herson has been released from his contract.

Genezaro Tribal Newsletter

A feature in our December newsletter, "Tribal Son Makes Good," contained some inaccuracies. Seymour Herson is not, in fact, a member of our tribe. His documents were forged. The article also said that Seymour would be attending Harvard in the fall. This is no longer true—his offer of admission has been rescinded.

The Genezaro Tribal Newsletter regrets the errors.

"Seymour? Jesus, how long have you been up here?"

"Ashley, if you tell *anyone*—"

"We're back to threats? Okay, fine, let's hear it. What are you going to do to me?"

I crawled out from under the water tower. My clothes were splotched with tar and my sweatshirt was damp from when it had rained the night before.

"Christ, buddy," she said. "Have you been hiding since yesterday?"

I nodded. I had snuck up the tunnel right after talking to Jessica. I had only meant to stay for a minute or two, to plan out what I was going to say to my parents. But it took me longer than expected to strategize. I knew I would start off with some small talk, to put them at ease. Something about the weather, like, "Guess summer's on its way," or, "Can you believe this rain?" That's as far as I had gotten.

"I saw Mr Hendricks talking to a reporter in the lobby," Ashley said.

"Oh my God."

"Relax, he's loving the attention."

She sat down next to me and flipped through a stack of tabloids. My face was on some of the covers.

"Man," she said. "You are busted."

"Yeah."

"You know what they're most upset about? The Indian thing."

I nodded.

"That one was pretty crazy."

I picked up the newspapers and felt their weight. How much

money did the Allagashes make from a stack this size? Ashley grabbed them and stuffed them into her bag.

"Nobody will care in a couple of days," she said. "Some lady in Omaha will drown her kids and people will forget all about you."

"God, I hope so."

She laughed.

"Come on," she said. "You've got to come down from here. This is ridiculous."

I shook my head stubbornly.

"What are you afraid of? You've already been caught."

I was concentrating on a nearby streak of tar to keep myself from crying. It wasn't working.

"Seymour, come on. What are you worried about?"

I wiped my eyes roughly with my sleeve.

"They're going to be mean to me."

"Who?"

"Everyone."

She nodded.

"Yeah."

I could hear the bell ringing in the distance, but I didn't budge.

"Hey," she said. "I'll be nice to you."

I looked at her suspiciously.

"*Why?*"

"Why not? It doesn't *cost* me anything. I mean it's not even my hot chocolate! I steal it from the cafeteria."

"Aren't you mad at me?"

"Yeah," she said. "Because you were a *jerk*. Not because you're not a real Indian. And I'm not mad anymore."

She handed me a mug.

"Here you go, Chunk-Style. Drink up."

"Ashley . . . I need to tell you something."

I took a deep breath.

"In eighth grade, when we were running for class president . . . me and Elliot, we fixed it so you would lose."

"I know about that."

"What?"

"I mean, I always assumed you cheated. But in case there was any doubt left in my mind . . ."

She rummaged through her bag and handed me a small gilded envelope. The wax seal was too smudged to read. But how many people had wax seals?

"When did Elliot send you that?"

She shrugged.

"A couple of months ago. I guess he thought I was a bad influence."

I stared at her in disbelief.

"But then why didn't you say anything? I mean, why'd you hang out with me anyway?"

"Because that was kid stuff, Seymour! I'm not a kid anymore. Are you?"

I swallowed.

"No."

I looked down at my lap.

"Ashley?"

"Yeah?"

I hesitated.

"Will you be my friend?"

When I looked up, she was smiling.

"I *am* your friend," she said. "Seymour, I'm your friend *already.*"

"Okay," I said. "I think I can come down."

I stood up and made my way toward the tunnel.

"Wait," she said. "Is it okay . . . I mean . . . can we just go the other way?"

I walked across the roof and grabbed her hand. She smiled.

"Let's never come back here," I said.

"Okay," she said.

And the two of us walked right out the door.

• • •

My parents must have been listening for the elevator, because they were waiting for me in the hall. My dad hooked his arms around me as soon as the doors slid open, while my mom shouted hysterically into the phone. They dragged me inside, shoved me onto the couch, and frantically examined my body for cuts and bruises. I was disheveled after my day as a fugitive, but my parents looked even worse. My mother's hair was wild and frazzled, and my dad's neck was crawling with scraggly hairs. I started to apologize—about hiding, about everything—but they both cut me off simultaneously.

"We can talk about all that stuff later," my dad said, untying the knots in my shoelaces.

My mom filled up the tub and I took my first bath in years. My face was still chalky with television makeup. I dunked my head underwater for as long as I could, and I could feel it peeling off in flakes.

I got dressed in an old, baggy Knicks jersey and made my way to the living room. There was brisket on the table and my parents were hunched over a box.

"It's Monopoly Night," my mom said, in as normal a voice as she could muster.

Restitution would start the following day and would take months. But first, my parents would allow themselves one night of domestic tranquility.

We ate in silence while my dad set up the board. The phone rang every couple of minutes. My dad would answer, mumble, "No comment," and then hang up. After seven or eight calls, he yanked the phone cord out of the wall.

I looked down at my plate. It was horrible to think about all of the humiliation my parents would have to deal with because of me.

My dad rooted around in the box until he found his wheelbarrow.

"Hey," he said. "Kiddo. You want to know something?"

I shrugged.

My father glanced at my mother, hesitated, and then cleared his throat.

"I cheat at Monopoly," he said.

I wasn't sure I had heard him correctly.

"Sorry," I said. "What?"

"I cheat at Monopoly," he repeated. "I've been doing it for years."

He threw his hands up in the air.

"There it is," he said. "I'm a full-grown man who cheats at a child's game."

"How?"

"I steal from the bank," he said. "That's why I always agree to be banker, so I can steal. I also steal from your mom."

"Jesus," I said. "Mom, can you believe this?"

"I've known about it for years," she said. "You know what's crazy? Sometimes he loses anyway."

My father nodded.

"I'm not good at Monopoly," he said.

"Wow," I said. "I never knew about that."

"Are you angry?" my dad asked.

"Well, a little, I guess. But you know . . . I'll get over it."

He reached across the board and grabbed my hand.

"You better," he said. "We're family."

The door buzzer rang sharply, and my parents both stood up.

"Jesus—"

"Don't tell me they looked up our *address*—"

"Guys!" I said. "It's okay. I forgot to tell you, I invited a friend over."

My mom's eyes widened with panic.

"Who?"

The doorbell rang. My parents were completely rigid as I walked across hall and opened the door.

"Hi," Ashley said.

"Hi," I said. "Mom, Dad? This is my friend Ashley."

"Oh!" my mom exclaimed. "Oh!"

"Nice to meet you!" my dad said. "You're just in time!"

He pulled a fourth chair up to the table and rummaged through the box for another game piece. Ashley was debating between the thimble and the car when I felt my phone vibrate against my leg. I took it out of my pocket, hesitated, and then slowly held it up to my ear.

"*Seymour!* Thank God you picked up!"

Ashley examined the car and then tossed it back into the box.

"You haven't been getting reception. Listen, we need to speak at once. It's urgent!"

She stuck her thimble on Go, and my father lined up the four pieces.

"I know I behaved rashly this week. I had to teach you a lesson—I know it was harsh, but it needed to be done. But you've got to understand, there's nothing I did that isn't totally reversible—as long as we act fast!"

My mother brought Ashley a plate, and my father served her a slice of brisket.

"Anyone can freeze in front of a camera! We can explain away every crime! Or better yet, frame someone! Multiple people! It doesn't matter! Within three weeks, a month, tops, I can get it all back for you—I've got journalists! I've got public officials! Seymour, are you listening to me?"

My parents looked up at me.

"This is just a blip on the timeline! In twenty years, we'll look back at this moment and laugh! Come over tonight. We'll start planning. I've already taken care of all the preliminaries— Harvard, Bishop House, the press—all I have to do is say go and they'll move like lightning! We can get it all back and more, Seymour! More!"

"Sweetie?" my mom asked. "Do you need to take it?"

"No," I said. "I don't."

I turned off the phone. Four gleaming pieces stood on Go, like runners jostling for position on a starting line. I picked up the dice and shook them over the five-hundred-dollar bill my father had placed on Free Parking.

Then I stopped.

"Is it okay if we play a different game?"

The four of us looked at each other in silent agreement.

"I'll get a puzzle," my mother said.

My father cleared away the Monopoly board, while my mother poked around in the closet. We only had one puzzle—a thousand piece jigsaw—buried in the back. The top of the box had gone missing, but she dumped out the pieces anyway.

"What's this a puzzle of?" Ashley said.

"I guess we'll find out," my dad said.

I reached for a piece and we started to put it all together.

PART THREE

Chance

*A*SHLEY AND I WERE BUYING supplies for a late-August road trip when we ran into Elliot Allagash. He was walking toward his limousine, shouting orders into his cell phone. A slovenly boy in baggy jeans and a wifebeater shuffled along beside him. I wasn't going to say hello, but Ashley called out his name.

Elliot looked up, swallowed, and closed his cell phone.

"Well," he said.

I followed Ashley down the sidewalk, and for the first time since we met, Elliot and I shook hands.

"This is Doug," Elliot said, gesturing at the oafish-looking boy standing behind him.

" 'Sup," Doug said. He held out a fist and Ashley and I bumped it.

"Doug's accompanying me to Harvard next month," Elliot announced, "despite a 2.3 grade point average and three arrests for public intoxication."

"Congratulations," I said.

Doug nodded.

"I'm going to smoke up behind that dumpster," he said.

"Very well," Elliot said.

He let out a long sigh as Doug lumbered off toward the alleyway.

"He might actually be retarded," Elliot said. "But I've gotten him into the greatest college in the world."

We all stood there for a moment in silence. Eventually, Ashley nudged me.

"So," I said. "How . . . um . . . did you do it?"

"It's none of your business," Elliot snapped.

There was a brief pause.

"Although if you must know, I blackmailed a bunch of professors and tricked them into thinking they were blackmailing one another."

He reached into his pocket and handed me a piece of paper.

"Here. Here's the chart I made to keep it all straight."

"Wow," I said. "That's really clever."

I looked around for Ashley, but she had walked over to a window display. She nodded at me and turned around.

I examined Elliot's chart; it was impossible to follow, but I could tell it had required an incredible number of hours to produce. I carefully refolded it and handed it back to him.

"So . . . um . . . how's your father?"

Elliot shrugged.

"Terry's leaving New York."

"Really?" I said. "Where's he going?"

"Massachusetts," he said, looking down at his feet. "Cambridge, actually."

"Oh yeah?"

"Yes. He purchased an historic building near Harvard, a former statehouse. Completely gutted it, to spite some local professors. Anyway, I'll be living there."

"That's nice that he moved all the way up there just to be closer to—"

"It's a coincidence," Elliot said. "His favorite hatmaker opened a haberdashery on Newbury Street. He followed him on a whim."

"Oh," I said. "Well that makes sense."

"Yes," Elliot said. "There are no good hatters in this city, so . . ."

"Of course."

Elliot nodded.

"We're . . . actually working on a little scheme right now," he said, "Terry and I."

"Really?"

"Yes. Terry came up with a plot to bypass my math and science requirements. It's quite artful—but very complicated. We'll have to put in a lot of hours to make it fly."

"I'm sure you guys will figure it out," I said.

"Yes. We're already well on our way."

Doug came out from behind the dumpster, walked past us and got into the limousine.

"I better go," Elliot said.

"Okay," I said. "Goodbye."

He got into his car, and it immediately sped down the avenue.

I walked over to Ashley, took her hand and started off in the other direction. We were halfway down the block when I looked over my shoulder. Elliot's limousine was disappearing down a hill, but I thought I could see his face poking out through the sunroof, gazing in my direction.

I remembered the rush of the wind in my hair as we bulleted down Park Avenue. A drink in my hand, the sun in my face, the entire world spread out beneath me! It was such a thrilling memory that I started to laugh out loud.

ACKNOWLEDGMENTS

This novel would not have been possible without the help of a shocking number of people:

My agent, Daniel Greenberg, believed in this project from my very first manic email. Over the past two years, he's given me valuable criticism and great advice, and talked me out of two separate panic attacks.

Jonathan Jao was a perfect editor. He backed me up whenever I was right and reasoned with me whenever I was wrong. His patience and insight dramatically improved this book and made me a better writer in the process.

My lawyer, Lee Eastman, took me on when I was a bewildered, unemployed twenty-two-year-old. I can't imagine navigating the past three years without his constant support and counsel. He's one of the first people I showed this novel to, and if he hadn't said "Go for it," I'm not sure that I would have.

My mother, the fabulous editor Gail Winston, read two early

drafts of this novel and gave me brilliant advice. Josh Koenigsberg helped me fill two separate plot holes, one of which I hadn't even spotted.

My dad, stepmom, and brother cheered me on throughout the writing process. And my friends heroically bore with me during the periods in which I was insane. There's not enough room to thank them all, but here are some: Azhar Khan, Monica Padrick, Josh Morgenthau, Brent Katz, Caitlin Petre, Steve Bender, Nick McDonell, Amanda Miller, Francesca Mari, David Herson, and Kathleen Hale.

Over the course of my short career, I've been lucky to collaborate with a lot of amazing writers. I've learned a lot from all of them and I wanted to list at least some here: Josh Koenigsberg, Bill Hader, Marika Sawyer, John Mulaney, Colin Jost, Seth Meyers, Bryan Tucker, Andy Samberg, Dan Menaker, Farley Katz, Zach Kanin, Andrei Nechita.

The writer Erik Kenward introduced me to the term "garbage animals." And my father deserves full credit for the "Where's the fish" story. He told it to me when I was eleven (and insists to this day that it is true!).

Thanks to Charles Dickens, P. G. Wodehouse, Evelyn Waugh, Roald Dahl, Terry Southern, David Sedaris, and the Simpsons.

Also: Evan Camfield, Simon M. Sullivan, Jennifer Huwer, Meghan Cassidy, Ben Wiseman, Caleb Beyers, Dustin Lushing, Lorne Michaels, Mike Shoemaker, Steve Higgins, Gregory McKnight, Shari Smiley, Forrest Church, Michael Hertzberg, and the park rangers of the Allagash Wilderness Waterway.

And finally . . .

Jake Luce provided criticism, advice, and encouragement at every stage of the creative process, from the novel's inception to its publication. I dedicated the book to him, but he probably belongs on the cover. I consider this book his as much as mine.

ABOUT THE AUTHOR

SIMON RICH has written for *The New Yorker, GQ, Mad, The Harvard Lampoon,* and other magazines. He is the author of two humor collections, *Free-Range Chickens* and *Ant Farm,* which was a finalist for the 2008 Thurber Prize for American Humor. He lives in Brooklyn and writes for *Saturday Night Live.*